He's getting married

To let anything come of this with a guy on the cusp of choosing a royal wife wouldn't do.

But...there was no actual woman in Malik's life, not even a name or a face, just a possibility. Yes, he would marry, and he would be out of Lucy's reach forever, but right now...

In an instant, her mind flew ahead and a series of events unraveled at supersonic speed.

A wedded Malik would mean the end of her job, whatever he said. He would surely have to spend a lot more time in Sarastan, and how would she fit into that scenario on a long-term basis? He might even emigrate completely: Would his aristocratic new wife really want to up sticks and move to London?

Lucy was facing the end of her career as she knew it, whether that end happened in a week, in a month or in agonizingly slow motion over a period of time.

And then...she would never see this man again.

But she was seeing him *now*, wasn't she?

Secrets of Billionaires' Secretaries

Unbuttoned by the off-limits boss...

Behind every man there's a great woman.
And behind Gabriel and Malik are their skillful
secretaries, Helen and Lucy. They keep not only
Gabriel's and Malik's nonstop schedules in check,
but the billionaires themselves!

But while Helen's and Lucy's abilities to put the
playboys in their place are unquestioned, their
newfound attraction to their bosses has them
questioning *everything*...

When Helen is mistaken as Gabriel's fiancée, they
are forced to maintain the wedding charade in order
to clinch a vital business deal!

A Wedding Negotiation with Her Boss

And might an unexpected return to Malik's kingdom
put Lucy in line for promotion—at the royal altar?

Royally Promoted

Both available now!

Royally Promoted

CATHY WILLIAMS

HARLEQUIN
PRESENTS

HARLEQUIN®
PRESENTS™

ISBN-13: 978-1-335-59363-4

Royally Promoted

Copyright © 2024 by Cathy Williams

Harlequin Enterprises ULC
22 Adelaide St. West, 41st Floor
Toronto, Ontario M5H 4E3, Canada
www.Harlequin.com

Printed in Lithuania

Recycling programs for this product may not exist in your area.

MIX
Paper | Supporting responsible forestry
FSC® C021394

Cathy Williams can remember reading Harlequin books as a teenager, and now that she is writing them, she remains an avid fan. For her, there is nothing like creating romantic stories and engaging plots, and each and every book is a new adventure. Cathy lives in London, and her three daughters—Charlotte, Olivia and Emma—have always been, and continue to be, the greatest inspirations in her life.

Books by Cathy Williams

Harlequin Presents

Desert King's Surprise Love-Child
Consequences of Their Wedding Charade
Hired by the Forbidden Italian
Bound by a Nine-Month Confession
A Week with the Forbidden Greek
The Housekeeper's Invitation to Italy
The Italian's Innocent Cinderella
Unveiled as the Italian's Bride
Bound by Her Baby Revelation

Secrets of Billionaires' Secretaries

A Wedding Negotiation with Her Boss

Visit the Author Profile page
at Harlequin.com for more titles.

CHAPTER ONE

'YOU'RE WET. WHY? Why are you soaking wet? You're also late.'

The door to Malik's office had been pushed open with its usual vigour and there she was, dripping on his pale-grey carpet, her blonde hair clinging to her in strands as she did her best to wring it out into semi-dried submission. He sat back in the leather chair, steepled his fingers and looked at his secretary with his head tilted to one side.

Lucy Walker, who had been working for him for a little over three years, was a force of nature. She was petite and curvy, with curly, bright blonde hair that had a will of its own, and a dimpled smile that had a disconcerting tendency to throw Malik off-track when he was taking her to task.

Right now was an excellent example.

Malik had long stopped asking himself how it was that she had stayed the course for as long as she had when, in every way, shape and form, she was precisely the sort of PA who normally wouldn't come close to being shortlisted for the high-powered role she occupied.

But she had shown up for the interview, impressed

him with her in-depth knowledge of negotiating the stock market, informed him that there was nothing she couldn't turn her hand to, smiled that dimpled smile and challenged him to set any task so that she could prove her worth.

Malik had duly given her ten minutes to work out projections for investing several million over several companies. She'd proven her worth in half the time. She was outspoken to a fault and was impressively immune to what, Malik knew, was a forbidding side to him that made most people think twice about saying anything of which he might disapprove. In every single walk of life, he was respected and feared in equal measure. But not by her.

She rid herself of her waterproof, which she dumped on the chair she occupied when in his office. The coat, too, was dripping onto his expensive carpet.

'Can you believe this weather, Malik? It's a disgrace. Why don't those overpaid people ever get the forecast right? No mention of a storm this morning when I switched on the telly—sunshine and showers!'

'Perhaps you should have paid more attention to the *showers* part of the weather report. It's after nine-thirty.'

'I would have texted, but my phone was low on juice. Still, I'm here now and ready to go! Lots of thoughts about that IT company you're looking to get hold of, by the way.'

'You need to go and get into some dry clothes.'

Lucy grimaced. 'That would involve a trip to the shops. I took the spare stuff I keep here back with me a couple of weeks ago and I completely forgot to replace them. I was bored of blues and greys. I thought that, with Christmas just round the corner, more festive colours might be in order.'

'We're in September.' Malik sighed heavily and sat back in the chair to look at her in brooding silence, before buzzing through to one of his other employees, who scuttled in at speed to stare with badly disguised laughter at his dripping secretary.

'Sir?'

'You need to go and get some dry clothes for Lucy,' he said, looking at Julia, who was secretary to one of the guys who worked for him. 'I don't care where. Put it on Robert's company card and be quick.'

'Malik…'

Malik looked at Lucy with an impatient frown. 'I need you here right now. I can't spare you for an hour hunting down a replacement outfit.'

'Duly noted.'

'Get one of the towels from the cloakroom and wrap it around you. I can't afford to have you off work with flu.'

'Trust me, flu is the last thing I want to have.'

Julia had hurried out, breathlessly promising to be back in under half an hour, which made Malik wonder how it was that his own secretary could be as stubborn as a mule when a snap of his fingers had every other person on the face of the earth jumping to attention.

'Off you go, Lucy. I have things to discuss with you of some importance, and time's moving along.'

Lucy ignored him to sit on the chair, casually pushing the wet waterproof off it and onto the ground.

'First, you deserve an explanation or else you're going

to be in a grumpy mood with me all day.' She dimpled. 'I thought I'd walk in this morning. It was so lovely and sunny, not a hint of those showers Carol on the telly mentioned at seven when I left home—and, actually, I need the exercise, if I'm honest with myself. I don't get nearly enough fresh air these days and—'

'Cut to the chase, Lucy.'

'So I headed off. Normally, it would have taken forty-five minutes, but then it clouded over, and forget about *showers*; this was a deluge. To top it all, the Tube drivers are on strike, which meant no Tube, and the buses were all packed out. Wasted nearly half an hour waiting at the bus stop. In the end, I had no option but to try and be as quick as I could on foot, but with the aforementioned deluge… You want to see the streets out there, Malik. They've turned into canals. We could be in Venice.'

'Did it occur to you at all to buy an umbrella?' He sincerely did not want to be amused.

'Not really, no. I kept thinking it would blow over. Anyway, it was all a bit chaotic.'

'I don't pay you handsomely to be chaotic.'

'Point taken.' She stood up, grimaced as she looked down at her wet outfit and told him that she'd be a minute, that the towel was a good idea and might warm her up.

'Can I get you a coffee on my way back?' she asked brightly.

'Just get yourself dried off, and you might just as well wait for Julia to get back with whatever she's got for you.' He dismissed her with a wave of his hand but continued to look at her as she hustled out of his office, closing the door behind her with a smart click.

This was not how he had anticipated starting the morning. Indeed, the entire day had kicked off to an unpredictable and nightmarish start, with his mother calling him at a little after four in the morning to inform him that his father had been rushed to hospital with a heart attack.

As usual, she had delivered the news coolly, calmly and without emotion. The only hint as to what was going on beneath the surface was the slight tremor in her voice when, after a moment's hesitation, she had told him that the doctors had been unable to confirm whether he would pull through. It was going to be a long night ahead.

'I'll come immediately,' Malik had said, already thinking ahead to the repercussions of his father's situation now staring him in the face.

They were not inconsiderable. Malik, at thirty-two, returned to his country of birth on a reasonably infrequent basis. Here in London, he ran the family house, where the vast wealth of his family was invested with military precision by a team of highly trained hedge-fund managers and investment bankers. He oversaw the lot of them, whilst handling his own pet projects: investments into green energy and property that would had made him a billionaire in his own right, regardless of his vast family fortune.

He liked it this way. Returning to Sarastan, where his parents lived in palatial splendour as dictated by their royal status, always came with the down side of their tacit disapproval about his marital status—or lack thereof. In their eyes, time was running out for him to continue the family name.

It was just the way it was.

Here in London, though, he could shove that inconvenient truth to the back of his mind. But now…?

He scowled as he waited for Lucy to return.

His father had been rushed to hospital and Malik knew exactly what that meant. His time for relaxing was over. Yes, he would still be able to live in London, with perhaps more frequent trips back to supervise the running of the various arms of the family businesses, and make sure the oil was still pumping and still being exported as it should be—not to mention all the other concerns that sheltered under the Al-Rashid umbrella. But the time to take a wife had come.

He wondered whether his mother would address the elephant in the room head-on, given the circumstances. She was a cold and regal woman, not inclined to indulge in conversations of a personal nature, always preferring him to get whatever message she wanted to convey via a combination of telling silence and disapproving asides.

His father was hardly any more communicative. Duty and obligation lay at the forefront of their rigidly controlled lives. With his father in hospital and facing an uncertain outcome, the weight of duty and obligation that they shouldered was bearing down fast on Malik, and he knew that he was stsanding at a crossroads, like it or not.

Lost in a sequence of unpleasant thoughts, he looked up to see his secretary framed in the doorway of his office, as dry as could be expected and in a different outfit: a thick grey skirt, a white blouse and a grey V-necked jumper.

Julia, he surmised, had been intentionally mischievous in the purchase and had managed to get hold of precisely the sort of clothes her friend would have made a point of shunning.

'Sit.'

'You're not still annoyed over my late arrival, are you?'

Malik watched as she tugged at the skirt and shoved up the arms of the jumper.

'Consider it forgotten, just so long as there isn't a repeat performance. You might want to check if the Tube is running next time you decide to walk to work and, while you're at it, you could also look at the weather forecast.'

'I'll definitely do the former but I won't bother with the latter. As I told you, no one mentioned a storm, and I could have happily coped with a light shower. You have a point, though. I might invest in an umbrella.'

She sat down, settled her laptop on the desk so that they were facing one another, flipped it open and proceeded to scrutinise him over the lid.

She had truly amazing eyes, cornflower-blue and fringed by the thickest, darkest lashes that contrasted spectacularly with the vanilla-blonde of her hair. She was intensely pretty, an impression that was compounded by the generosity of her curves and the way she dimpled whenever she smiled.

'You'll be impressed to hear,' she was saying now,

'That not only have I sorted out all those back reports you gave me on Friday, but I've also managed to get through to the bio-fuel company you're looking at reaching out to and persuaded them to forward me their latest balance of accounts. That's in addition to the tech company you're thinking of acquiring.'

'You spent the weekend working?'

'A couple of hours, that's all. No need to thank me.'

Malik hesitated.

That was the first inkling Lucy had that the day was not going to go to plan.

Staring at him, at the sharp lines of his incredibly beautiful face, she felt momentarily disconcerted because hesitation really didn't feature in his database.

She had been working for him for three years and she could say, in all honesty, that she had never met anyone as focused, as single-minded, as crazily sharp or as utterly self-assured as the guy sitting opposite her. He could be ruthless, forbidding and cold but, for Lucy, those traits were eclipsed by other, more compelling ones.

She knew that he scared a lot of people but, oddly, he didn't intimidate *her* and he never had—even when she had walked into his office all those years ago, having made it through the gruelling preliminary interviews, to face the final hurdle for the job she had hoped to secure.

He had thrown her a challenge, something to do with the stock market, and she had met the challenge in half the allotted time, tempted to ask him if he had anything harder up his sleeve. Just as she was leaving, he'd asked her why she thought she deserved the job when there were more qualified candidates desperate for it. She hadn't batted an eyelid. She'd smiled and told him that that was a question that wouldn't even cross his mind in a year's time because she would have long since proved herself.

Lucy knew that, whether he would ever agree with her or not, her ability to answer him back and speak her mind went a long way to earning his respect...*whether she had a university degree or not.*

Speaking her mind was something that came naturally to her. Sandwiched between four sisters, speaking her mind was the only tool she'd had ever been able to use to get heard.

As the only non-graduate in her entire family, and that included her parents, she'd had to find her voice from very early on to make sure she wasn't squashed by her much more academic sisters with their strident opinions, all of whom wanted to be one step ahead of the others.

A sprawling family of girls had come with other disadvantages, along with the amazing up sides, but being invisible had never been one of those disadvantages.

'You're looking at me as though you want to tell me something but can't figure out how,' she said now, direct as always, even though just voicing those thoughts made her feel a little uneasy. 'You're not about to sack me, are you?'

'I'm not about to sack you.'

'Thank goodness. I couldn't face jumping back into the job market. It's a shark pit out there.'

'I had a call very early this morning, Lucy. My mother telephoned to tell me that my father has been rushed to hospital—his heart. He's had a triple bypass, and they're waiting overnight to see whether the operation has been successful.'

'Oh. My. Goodness…' She half-stood, hesitated, then sat back down. She knew that she was emotional, but her boss was not, and a hug was the last thing he would welcome.

Thinking about it, hugging him was also something that made a curious tingle feather up and down her spine.

'I'm so sorry, Malik,' she said with genuine sympathy. 'You must be devastated. How is your mother taking it?'

'As well as can be expected.'

'You'll want to think about going over, I suppose. Do you want me to arrange a flight for you?' Her voice was uncharacteristically subdued.

'Yes. I'll have to return, and possibly for a matter of several weeks. I'll have to see how the land lies, and naturally I'll be returning to London, but in the interim arrangements will have to be put in place while my father recuperates—and that is if there's no worst-case scenario.'

'Worst-case scenario?'

'If he doesn't pull through,' Malik said bluntly and was unsurprised when she paled.

She was as transparent as a pane of glass and generous when it came to expressing her feelings. After months spent dissuading her from that weakness, because emotionalism frankly got on his nerves, he had now given up. Maybe he'd just got used to it, but it didn't get on his nerves in her case.

'Oh, don't even think of going there, Malik. The most important thing you can do now is remain positive. It's called the laws of attraction. At least, I think that's what it's called. It's all about positivity making good outcomes. What can I do? I'm so, so sorry.'

'These things happen, Lucy,' he said flatly. 'And, for the record, I'll dispense with the mumbo-jumbo nonsense. I'm a realist and I know that preparations will have to be made for all eventualities. However, we won't dwell on that. Let's return to the fact that I'm going to be out of the country for quite some time.'

'Yes, let's.' Lucy was trying to work out how the place would run without him there but, then again, he was a master at delegation and had the sort of well-oiled, high-level team that could march onwards without supervision, such was their level of excellence and the depth of their loyalty to their paymaster.

Which begged the question...*where did she fit in to all of this?*

Which instantly brought her back to that moment of hesitation she had seen shadow his face earlier. He might not be sacking her, but was he going to give her a little reduced-pay time off? Lucy sincerely hoped not. Despite being surrounded by high powered sisters, she was on a par with them earnings-wise, and had been furiously putting money aside to get her own place.

She knew she was proving a point because she had no degree. Proving that she could be a success at what she did, because everyone had had their say when she'd ditched university without warning. One minute her bags had been packed for Durham, and the next minute they'd been unpacked and she'd turned her back on what her entire family had expected of her. Goodbye maths and economics course, hello technical college in Exeter, as far from the family home in leafy Surrey as she'd been able to get.

No one could fathom the reason why, and she hadn't confided, because she had never been more alone than at that very point in time in her lovely, noisy family.

How could she have told any of them about the fool she had been? How could she have admitted that she had fallen head over heels for a smooth-talking charmer who had turned her head, strung her along and then ditched her the minute she'd told him that they'd made a very costly mistake?

How could she ever have borne the mortification of telling any of the family that she had accidentally fallen pregnant? Two of her sisters were married with kids. Their pregnancies had been meticulously planned. Noisy debates had abounded over the years about girls who had unplanned pregnancies.

How on earth did that happen?

How hard was it to get hold of the pill?

A week after she'd been ditched, she had miscarried. She'd barely been pregnant and yet the pain had been immense. She'd turned her back on all the expectations lying on her shoulders and she'd started walking down a different road. She hadn't regretted it. It had led her to the most interesting job imaginable, working for the most interesting man imaginable, with a stupendous pay cheque and none of the constant stress her sisters seemed to face in their chosen fields of medicine and law.

A pay cheque she had grown accustomed to. At the moment she rented, which was very expensive to do in London, even where she lived in her small box on the third floor of a mansion block, the saving grace being the fact that it was in an okay part of North London.

So, with Malik departing for faraway shores for an indeterminate length of time… Well, from where she was sitting, the future was beginning to look far from rosy. All the managers there had their own dedicated secretaries. The intense nature of their jobs demanded it. Was she about to be tacked on to someone else's desk, fetching cups of coffee while Malik disappeared on a one-way ticket to Sarastan?

She was highly imaginative and now, as she stared at him, for once in complete silence, her imagination was hurtling in free fall. She was further dismayed by that hesitation on his face again and, instead of doing what she would normally have done, instead of flatly asking him what was going on, she found herself biting her lip. Sometimes to ask a question risked getting an answer you didn't particularly want to hear.

'It's inevitable, I'm afraid, and not at all welcome.'

'I can imagine, although I'm sure your parents will really enjoy having you back with them. I'm confident your dad will be released from hospital and be fighting fit in no time at all.' She wondered what it would be like, not waking in the morning to the thought of going in to work, where Malik would be waiting with a list as long as his arm of things for her to do. Her heart skipped a beat at a sudden sense of loss.

Malik raised his eyebrows. 'Positivity, yes. I got it the first time. No need to revisit the theme. You'll no doubt be wondering where you fit into this picture.'

Lucy reddened. 'It's a tough time for you,' she said gruffly, 'And where I fit in isn't important. The most important thing is for you to be out there for your family. They need you.'

'A generous sentiment. Here's where you fit in—I will have a great deal of work to do out there. Naturally, I'll make sure that everything is in place here to cover my absence, and remote work is largely trouble-free, but I will still have to devote considerable time to making sure everything over here ticks along without any hitches. Not just this office, but as you know there are a lot of ongoing deals at the moment, and taking my eye off the ball isn't going to do.'

'I suppose not, although…'

'Although…?'

'I could do my best to keep things ticking over if you assign someone to temporarily take your place. You know how good I am at self-motivating and I know most of those deals going through like the back of my hand. Ask me any question about any of them and I'll be able to give you an answer. I'm obviously not saying that as a *long-term* solution it would work—that would be crazy. But in the short term, I could do my best.'

'I hate to break this to you, Lucy, but, good as you are, I am irreplaceable.'

Lucy's eyebrows shot up. 'You have a very high opinion of yourself.' She dimpled and Malik returned the smile with raised eyebrows and one of his own.

He'd been wired since his mother had called him. Yes, he was concerned for his father's health, but beyond that the unravelling ramifications of what had happened had initiated a series of conclusions, none of which were particularly pleasant and all of which would have to be dealt with.

But here, with Lucy, he felt himself relax. The woman was a tonic, with her breezy irreverence. That was something he reluctantly had to concede.

'How well you know me,' Malik drawled but the half-smile left his lips as quickly as it had appeared and he stood up and strolled towards the window.

Lucy's eyes followed him.

He was a thing of beauty, she mused. It never failed to impress her. Everything about him was stunning, from the chiselled perfection of his harsh, arrogant features to the grace and symmetry of his long, muscular body.

He was six-four and there was not an ounce of wasted fat to be seen. He was all sinew, muscle and well-honed physical perfection. If all else failed, a career in modelling awaited.

He was intensely private and, despite the fact that Lucy had worked for him for over three years, she had in fact only ever met one of his girlfriends, a judge, and, she had later learnt, the youngest woman ever to have taken silk.

From that one encounter, Lucy had formed a picture

in her head of the sort of women he favoured: tall, elegant, career-driven beauties who had powerful jobs and dressed in snappy, sharp designer clothes that were immaculately tailored and never prone to mundane things like creasing or the occasional coffee stain. Women who definitely wouldn't go with festive colours in September.

He was a guy who liked sophistication, beauty and could easily get both. Why had he never married? She had no idea, but rich guys played the field...didn't they? And he wasn't old by any means, so he had years left in him to play in whatever fields took his fancy.

He might be a million light years away from the nightmare she had once dated, but Lucy knew that, however seriously sexy he was, and however often her disobedient eyes were inclined to stray in his direction, she could never consider him anything other than her gorgeous boss, because he was a guy who couldn't commit.

Heartbreak, and the loneliness and disillusionment that had come with it, had taught her that the one thing in life she wanted in a man was commitment. She didn't care about anything else because nothing else mattered. The guy who was willing to commit was the guy who was willing to give his heart, and without that what was left was some chump happy to use a woman for as long as it suited him before dumping her by text.

That would never be Malik's style. She knew him well enough by now to know that. But he still wasn't into long-term commitment. So she allowed her eyes to stray, and now and again her imagination went for the ride, but that was as far as it would ever get.

Which was all moot anyway, because he would never

spare a glance her way. She idly thought of her friend Helen, now happily married to her billionaire boss and just expecting their first baby, and had to reluctantly concede that at times the exception proved the rule.

Her mind drifted. Helen was contained and *mysterious*. They had been out many times together, and Lucy had always noticed the way guys had surreptitiously glanced at her friend, sizing her up and taking her in. Of course, Helen never seemed to notice, but at first she had still been wrapped up in memories of George and her own disappointment there, and then without even realising it wrapped up in the whole business of falling for her boss.

Unlike her friend, Lucy was the opposite of mysterious. There was no room for mystery when she'd grown up in a family of vocal, assertive people. Mystery, in the environment in which she had grown up, would have been the equivalent of disappearing. Her dad often joked that he had to make an appointment to get a word in edgeways, which made her think of Malik and his dad, and how calmly and coolly he'd relayed the facts about his hospitalisation.

'Are you paying a scrap of attention to what I am saying, Lucy?'

Lucy blinked and surfaced to find her boss frowning at her. He was backlit by the thin, fading, last-of-the-summer sun filtering through the windows, a dark, looming silhouette that momentarily took her breath away.

'Sorry, I was a million miles away.'

'You need to focus. I'm talking about your immediate future and how what's happened is going to have an impact on you.'

Lucy straightened, suddenly tense. She tucked her unruly blonde hair behind her ears and stared down at the desperately boring clothes her work colleague had decided to choose for her. She liked bright colours. It seemed appropriate that she was now wearing drab-as-dishwater clothes for an occasion like this, one in which she was obviously going to find the comfortable course of her life thrown off-course for reasons that had nothing to do with her.

'I'm focused,' she said quietly. 'You know I'm good at focusing even if it may not always seem that way.'

'I will have to leave immediately—probably by tomorrow evening. I've arranged a board meeting with my ten top guys to fill them in.'

'And me?'

'This is where it may be a bit tricky.' He raked his fingers through his hair and again that off-putting hesitation was back on his face.

'I wish you'd just say what you have to say,' Lucy finally said with her customary forthrightness. 'Since when do you make a habit of holding back? I'm a grown woman. I can take it. You told me I'm not going to get the sack because you have to return to Sarastan, so where does that leave me? Am I about to be demoted to office junior, is that it? Wearing a uniform, sweeping the floors and making sure the place is locked last thing?'

Malik ignored her flight of imagination, which he was used to. 'The favoured option is for you to accompany me, Lucy. I won't be able to get hold of anyone who will be able to work as efficiently alongside me as you. You're familiar with multiple takeovers, and you know the ropes when it comes to dealing with clients.'

'You want me to come with you?'

Malik tilted his head to one side and strolled back towards his desk.

'I appreciate,' he said gravely, 'That this is going to be massively inconvenient for you, and I'll naturally ensure that you are compensated accordingly.'

Lucy stared at him in silence as her brain shifted gear and began travelling down an altogether different route.

'You said you had no idea how long you would be away,' she reminded him slowly.

'It's a tough call. My father, presuming he pulls through this, might recover quickly or it might go slower than expected. I can't put a timeline on it for obvious reasons, which makes it even more inconvenient for you. I've given this thought, and I'll formally sign a contract that allows you to bail should you find the conditions onerous.'

'Conditions onerous... The mind boggles.'

'You have an active life here,' Malik said bluntly. 'You'll lose that immediately should you accept my offer.' He paused. 'I'm not entirely sure whether that active life involves a boyfriend,' he mused, narrowing his eyes and staring at her. 'Does it? And, if so, would that be a temporary loss you would be willing to endure? Like I said, I don't know for sure how long my presence will be required in Sarastan. It's not just being there while my father recovers but in terms of sorting out my family's business affairs. I'm hoping it's weeks rather than months, and of course I'll be going to and from London, I imagine, but I can't give you a precise timeline. Right now, everything is up in the air.'

'I… I…'

'I'd like to give you time to consider my proposition, Lucy. I know this has been thrown at you out of the blue. But, in this instance, time is of the essence. I would propose you make arrangements to join me within the week.'

'Within the *week*?'

'If you rent, all rent would be covered until you return so that you don't jeopardise where you live. If you own, all mortgage payments will be handled. All bills will be met. Additionally, as compensation, I'll treble your pay for the duration of your time in my country.'

'*Treble?*'

'You're parroting me.'

'Can you blame me? My thoughts are all over the place.'

'Moving along, you'll also find your bank account substantially increased to cover incidentals such as appropriate clothing, shopping, beauty treatments…or whatever else it is that you do with your money.'

'Does it look as though I spend lots of money on beauty treatments?' Lucy said absently, while her mind continued to somersault. 'If I did, my hair would know how to do what it was told.'

'You haven't answered my question, Lucy. Is there a man in your life? Someone who might prevent you from disrupting your routine here?'

'Possibly,' she said airily. 'However, I should say that,

were there such a man, I would never allow him to dictate how I chose to handle my life.'

'Patient guy, were such a man to be in your life.'

'In this day and age, Malik, men don't decide what women do. It's all about equal partnership.' She saw that he was smiling, amused, yet something in her shivered at the thought of this big, powerful man being protective of his woman. 'What if I choose not to go out there?'

'Naturally, your job would be safe,' Malik said briskly. 'But in all honesty there wouldn't be much for you to do here, as this is an intense group of people with dedicated PAs. Of course, you could while away the hours sweeping floors, as you say, but actually you would be put on temporary leave of absence until such time as I returned to London. Obviously, after a certain period of time full pay may no longer be appropriate, which we can discuss, but you would still be compensated adequately and your job would be held for you, unless I decide to limit my time in London and take up full residence in Sarastan.'

'What's the likelihood of that?' She paled as a void opened up at her feet.

'Who knows?' Malik shrugged. 'I can speculate but there's no reliable crystal ball to hand.'

There was an ominous note to that suggestion that sent chills down Lucy's spine. She knew that she got away with a lot when it came to her brilliant, charismatic boss but the truth was, there was an iron fist concealed within the velvet glove, and she was getting the uneasy impression that there were definite limits to how much he would indulge her.

Theirs was a healthy trade-off. He allowed her outspoken irreverence and, in return, she gave him the benefit of her amazing talent, which involved not only the number-crunching she was exceptionally good at but a real gift at communicating with people, so that he could leave many jobs involving important clients for her to handle at her discretion. She worked very hard, not to mention over and beyond without question.

Trade-offs, however, were not set in stone. And what would she be sacrificing if she accompanied him to his country for a few weeks? Lots of stuff with her family...movies, dinners out and pub lunches now and again with her friends...

'But where would I stay?' she asked with genuine curiosity. 'Would there be some sort of routine there? How would it all work? What would I do in my spare time?'

'A routine will be established when we get there. On the work front, with some disturbances given the situation, things will mirror what happens here. The scenery might change, Lucy, but the job will remain the same.' He smiled wryly. 'Trust me, Sarastan is an extremely wealthy country and I am an extremely wealthy man within it. I'd go so far as to say that my family are...of much elevated status. As such, you will find that your life will lack nothing when it comes to creature comforts.'

'Much elevated status? What does that mean?'

'Of royal lineage,' Malik expanded. 'On a more practical front, you may have to adapt your dress code to accommodate the heat and...' he paused '...you might find that my family...my parents...are painfully reserved.

It may take a while for them to become accustomed to your, er, ebullience…'

Lucy got the message loud and clear and she burst out laughing…because fair was fair.

'I'll do my best to curb my enthusiasm.' She grinned.

'You can be your usual exuberant self when you're with me,' Malik conceded wryly. 'In fact, it would be odd dealing with a *quiet* you. So, what's it to be, Lucy?'

'Okay. I'll come. Is that all there is I need to know?'

Now that she had made her decision, she was already thinking ahead to what would be a wonderful adventure, a few weeks away from the pleasant predictability of her life. She wouldn't start extrapolating to anything beyond that. There was no point trying to cross bridges that weren't even on the horizon yet.

'I'll email you with the details of what you'll need to know, pack, and expect, for that matter.' He frowned and then, as he was about to return to the business of work, said, 'Just one more thing I suppose you should know…'

'What's that?'

'The time has come for me to marry. Finding a wife will probably be something else on the agenda whilst I am over there.'

CHAPTER TWO

WHAT? A WIFE? You're going to be finding a wife? Wait! What?

In receipt of that shocking postscript casually tacked on to the end of the conversation, Lucy's jaw dropped to the ground.

She had a million and one questions to ask him but, before she could get the first one out, he held up his hand, turned his attention to his computer and informed her that there was a hell of a lot to get through before he left, and three hours of valuable working time had already been squandered because of her late arrival.

'Yes, but...'

'But...?'

'You have to find a *wife*, Malik? As in, see what's available at the nearest department store? Maybe have a look in the cosmetics department? Who *does* that?'

In response, his eyebrows had shot up and he had said, wryly, 'Actually, Lucy, that aspect of my trip back to Sarastan will be the one that affects you the least. I only mentioned it because you'll obviously be around and there's no point having you indulge in colourful guessing games, should you be confronted with the situation as it unfolds.'

'The situation *as it unfolds*? Will you be conducting interviews for the post?'

'I haven't given much thought to the how the process will be negotiated. Now...back to those reports on Thompson and the bio-fuel company I have my eyes on...'

And that was that.

She spent the remainder of the day eaten up with curiosity.

Why was he looking for a *wife*? He could have anyone he wanted. One snap of his fingers, and there would be a queue of eligible women forming down the road. So, why go to the trouble of practically interviewing, for want of a better word, for the role? Whatever had happened to love?

It occurred to her that she knew precious little about Malik's family and personal life. While she made a habit of saying exactly what was in her head, he was careful with what he revealed, which, when she thought about it, was precious little.

By the end of the very long day, during which she barely had time to break for lunch, Lucy was spent, partly from working non-stop and partly because being eaten up with curiosity was an exhausting business and took a lot of energy.

'Right; enough. I think we've covered all we're going to be able to cover for the day.' This from Malik as he appeared at her desk to stare down at her as she furiously flicked through various open screens on her laptop, link-

ing multiple reports and working at breakneck speed
to cover the workload he had left her to get through in
record time.

Lucy sat back and looked up and up and up at him.

'Very good.'

'I beg your pardon?' She arched her eyebrows and
looked directly into amused dark eyes.

'You've done very well today. One hundred percent
focus, even though I know you must have many questions to ask.'

'I hardly know where to begin with them, now that
you mention it.'

'I'm sure, and they'll all be answered. It's…' he
glanced at his watch '…a little after six. Why don't I
take you somewhere for an early dinner and you can ask
away? It's a temporary lifestyle change for you but it's a
significant one. You need to get to Sarastan with a clear
head and as little apprehension as possible.'

'Right now?'

Malik frowned. 'Right now, what?'

'Dinner.'

Lucy stood up, glanced down at her disorganised
desk, stuck a pen in the flowerpot she used as a con-
tainer and decided that further work to neaten her work
area would have to wait for another day.

'Right now, Lucy.'

'I can't.'

'Why not?'

'I hate what I'm wearing and I refuse to be seen in it
anywhere, unless it's on a bus heading back home, pref-
erably behind dark shades and wearing a wig. Remind

me to think up something clever to get back at Julia for this little trick of hers.'

Malik shook his head, looked to be on the verge of saying something and then raked his fingers through his hair.

'Lucy, it's now or never. I have things to do and I haven't got time for you to go back to wherever you live and change into something you feel more comfortable wearing. Besides, those colours... Believe it or not, those are the colours largely worn by the working population in the City.'

'All very dismal, boring people.' She grinned. 'With the exception of everyone working in these offices. Okay, could you at least give me ten minutes to freshen up? And it's in Swiss Cottage, by the way.'

'What is?'

'Where I rent.'

'Ten minutes. I'll meet you in the foyer on the ground floor.'

Malik watched as she began gathering her various belongings. She was right. There was a vibrancy about her that didn't work well with greys, blacks and navy-blues although, in fairness, they did work when it came to providing contrast with the bright-vanilla blonde of her hair which had now dried into a waterfall of corkscrew curls falling over her shoulders, almost to her waist.

The women he dated tended to be tall, angular and brunette with controlled hair and, yes, a predilection for all those colours his secretary had scorned. Just for a fleeting moment, he narrowed his gaze to look at her and was caught by the softness of her skin, the way her hair fell in its unruly tangle as she bent to reach for her bag, which had been dumped on the ground next to her chair, and the swing of heavy breasts just about outlined under the top Julia had decided to buy for her colleague, tongue no doubt very firmly in cheek as she'd made her choice.

Then he turned away with a dark flush and began heading for the door that led out to the main open-plan office with its towering greenery, carefully positioned glass partitions, sleek wood and metal desks.

Lucy spotted him as soon as the lift disgorged her and its other eight occupants into the grand marble foyer that housed Malik's elite, high-powered workforce. They occupied two floors of a towering glass building in the City. Two floors where the elite of the elite handled more billions than anyone would ever come close to guessing.

He was sitting on one of the grey chairs clustered round a circular glass table and was frowning at whatever he was reading on his phone. His long legs were stretched out and he had undone the top three buttons of his white, hand-tailored shirt.

She stopped dead in her tracks and stared for a few seconds. Her heart picked up speed. She had signed up to going away with this guy for weeks and she had no real idea what that was going to entail, aside from the fact that it would, supposedly, work as usual.

With the small technicality of him interviewing a suitable wife. So, in other words, not really *working as usual*, was it? Because, as he had pointed out, she was going to be around, so whatever fascinating interview techniques he got up to, presumably she would be in the vicinity with a bird's eye view of what was going on.

Maybe he foresaw these interviews being conducted during working hours. She pictured herself scurrying around with cups of tea and coffee for an array of women sitting outside his office, sprucing up their CVs and anxiously rehearsing answers to possible questions.

He glanced up suddenly and she blushed, fussed with her skirt and made her way over to him as he simultaneously rose to his feet, six foot four of sinful perfection.

'Right. Ready for me to answer those tons of questions you have?' He smiled.

'I should have made a list.'

'I can't imagine you need a list to fire away, Lucy. I've phoned ahead and there's a table waiting for us at the French bistro a couple of streets away. I've made sure to ask them to sit us somewhere relatively quiet.'

'Don't you need to reserve that place months in advance?' Lucy fell into step, very much aware of him next to her as they left the glass building and emerged onto streets that were busy with after-work crowds keen to make the most of whatever fine weather was left of summer, which wouldn't be much.

Where was she going to live? Was she even going to like it there? What if she ended up lonely and miserable, hiding away in her bedroom?

'I can hear you thinking, Lucy,' Malik murmured with wry amusement, leaning down so that she could feel the warmth of his breath against her ear which made her shiver.

'Can you blame me?'

'I'd be surprised and disappointed if you didn't have anything to ask.'

Lucy was frowning and going through a veritable hornet's nest of scenarios which had been noticeably absent when she had airily accepted his offer a few hours ago.

The adventure aspect was beginning to nudge elbows with the fear factor, but she reminded herself that it was hardly going to be a life change set in stone, signed in blood and lasting years. Furthermore if she *did* end up feeling miserable and lonely—which was highly un-likely, because why would she?—then she could always leave. She wasn't going to be manacled to the office desk, after all.

The bistro was already heaving by the time they got there but they were ushered to a quiet table at the very back of the room.

'I've never been here before.' She looked around her appreciatively. It was very modern with clean lines, a black-and-white tiled floor and interesting framed black-and-white photos on the walls of places and people she didn't recognise but felt she probably should.

Her mind was pleasantly diverted from her rising stress levels until her gaze landed squarely on the guy sitting opposite her, at which point she remembered that this was the very guy she had agreed to accompany abroad for an indefinite period of time.

'Wine?'

When Lucy looked, it was to find that a bottle of Chablis had been delivered to the table, along with some nibbles in a pewter dish.

'Sure.'

'Shall we order before the inquisition begins?'

'It's not going to be an inquisition.'

'I reserve judgement. The fish is extremely good here. How is it you've never been when it's ten minutes away from the office?'

'Perhaps you haven't checked the prices,' Lucy said kindly. 'Slightly out of my price range for a quick bite after work.'

'You're extremely well paid, Lucy. I personally handle all your salary increases and bonuses.'

'Yes, well…'

'And, in case I've never told you, you deserve every penny of those salary increases and bonuses.'

'Thank you, Malik. I appreciate that.'

Malik grinned. 'Now.' He sat back and flung his arms wide without taking his eyes off her face. 'Fire away.'

'What's it like?'

'What's what like?'

'Sarastan. Where you live. What's it like?'

'Relatively small and extremely wealthy.'

'Is that it?'

'It's largely desert, but there is some truly exquisite scenery and the surrounding sea is beautiful. We have breath-taking skyscrapers, world-class restaurants, luxury shopping malls and awe-inspiring houses.'

'Why did you leave?'

'Come again?'

'If it's so fantastic, why are you living in dreary London with its grey skies and pollution?'

Malik's gaze cooled. 'Not pertinent to your temporary posting over there, Lucy. You need to stick to the brief.'

Lucy reddened, a retort springing to her lips, but then it hit her that he was absolutely right.

This was an unusual situation, which didn't mean that she wasn't still his employee, paid by him to do a job. She was here to ask practical questions that would be relevant to her life over there, not delve into his personal thoughts on anything. Boundary lines existed between them for a very good reason and she would have to make sure that they didn't get crossed. What Malik's private life looked like was none of her business any more than it hers was his business.

'Where will I be living?' She changed direction, and then took time out to inspect the menu which had been brought to their table, quickly making a choice, although she hardly paid attention to what was there.

'I'll make sure that something very comfortable is sorted out for you.' He looked at her pensively. 'I usually stay with my parents when I'm over there,' he mused, thinking aloud. 'But, given the circumstances, I think I'll change that routine. In fact...'

'In fact...?' Lucy sat back as a basket of bread was brought to the table along with some very interesting-looking butter. She hesitated and, when she glanced at him, he waved at the bread and told her to tuck in.

'I won't, actually,' Lucy said politely. 'I'm not a bread person.' It occurred to her that this was the first time she had ever been to dinner with Malik on a one-to-one basis. Yes, they had shared a meal on the run, something brought to the office when they'd happened to be working late on a deal with a deadline, but dinner at a fancy place like this? Never.

Suddenly self-conscious, she primly placed her hands on her lap and sat back.

'Really? That flies in the face of the many baguettes you've bought from the deli on the corner at lunchtime.'

Lucy was suddenly stung by that remark. What did he really think of her, she wondered, apart from being a whizz at what she did? Did he find her too talkative, too mouthy? An open book without any interesting nooks and crannies? She was hardly an enigma, was she?

Out of nowhere, she thought of her sisters. They'd all followed in the footsteps of their dad, while she never did as she was told, feet firmly planted in the footsteps of their mum. She'd taken that break-up all those years ago so hard, and she had never really forgotten it, had never forgotten the trauma of that early miscarriage and the horror of being ditched like a sack of old junk that had seen better days. It had wreaked havoc with her self-confidence, and at the time had made her look in the mirror and wonder if she was as awful as she felt.

'You're upset,' Malik said quietly. 'I'm sorry if I offended you with that remark.'

'Offended? Me?' Lucy loosed a brittle laugh but she had to desperately blink back the urge to cry. 'As if. Where are you going to put me when I come over? You still have to answer that.'

Malik looked at her in silence for a few seconds, long

enough for her to squirm, but she maintained eye contact, her chin tilted at a defiant angle.

She was saved by the arrival of her fish course, which allowed her to break eye contact and focus on the turbot on her plate. Her heart was thudding inside her. He'd apologised; he had seen the way she had reacted to his perfectly innocent, amusing banter and that, somehow, felt worse than if he hadn't said anything.

Did he pity her, feel sorry for her? Lucy knew that her imagination was playing tricks on her and she breathed in deeply and began to nibble at the food.

What did it matter what Malik thought of her? The most important thing was that she impressed him with her ability to do the job she was paid to do.

Did it matter whether he saw her as a *woman* or not? No!

She eyed him surreptitiously from under her lashes and accepted that anyone as beautiful as he was would really be unable to see her as anything other than the woman who worked for him. Guys who could have any woman they desired weren't the sort of guys who'd give her a second glance.

She forced a smile and made a few noises about the excellent quality of the food.

'So? You were saying?'

Malik finally picked up the thread of the conversation as he dug into the food on his plate. 'I think I'll use one of the family properties to house us.'

'Sorry?' Fork on the way to her mouth, Lucy froze as she digested this.

'It would make sense.'

'On what planet would it make sense?' The words were out before she could take time to think about it. 'Malik, I'm not sharing *a house* with you!'

'Why not?'

'Because…because I'm *not*!'

'You shock me,' Malik murmured, looking down as he calmly carried on eating. 'What's there not to like about the idea? We'll be working together, and it would certainly do away with the aggravating chore of making our way into the capital every day.'

'That's not going to work, Malik. No way.'

'I'm very well trained in all domestic settings,' Malik told her mildly. 'Despite my privileged background, I find I'm generally capable of tidying up after myself in the absence of anyone else to do it for me and, at a push, have actually created one or two edible meals for myself.'

'Forget it!'

Her cheeks were hot and her pulses were racing. Disturbing images were flying through her head at dizzying speed. They involved the two of them in close quarters, bumping into one another in search of the kitchen late at night for a glass of water, sharing dinners, lunches and breakfasts, settling down to watch telly in the living room…

Her heart was on the verge of packing up altogether when she slowly noticed that he was finding it hard to control his laughter.

'What?' Lucy snapped, blinking her way back to reality.

'Calm down, Lucy,' he said gently. 'I know what's

going through your head, and there's nothing to get over-excited about here. The family residence is a palace of quite sizeable proportions. It'll be convenient, because it's close enough to my parents' place for me to visit regularly to check my father's progress as and when. It'll also be big enough for you to have your own quarters, which will be in a completely different wing to where I will be staying. You'll even have your own garden where you can relax any time you want. I already have various rooms kitted out for office purposes, and naturally there will be staff on hand to take care of all our daily requirements. You'll find that you won't have to lift a finger.

'If it's any consolation, I've used the place hundreds of times for conferences that have involved people from different countries having to power-work on something and needing a place to stay for a few days at a time.'

Lucy stared at him and tried to sift through this baffling array of information, finally settling on, 'Palace? We'll be staying in a palace? When you say *palace*…?'

'You'll get the picture soon enough.'

'And when you say *staff*…?'

'You won't have to cook or clean or generally think about doing anything aside from working and relaxing.'

'I can't see myself relaxing in a place where I won't know anyone.'

'You'll know me.'

'You're my boss, Malik. It's completely different.'

'Is this your way of telling me that you're having second thoughts?'

'No. I said I'd come and I will. I'm just voicing a few perfectly valid concerns. A girl has to be prepared...'

'I could introduce you to some of my relatives who are your age.'

'You have brothers? Sisters?'

'I have cousins.'

'But no siblings.'

'We seem to be going a little off-piste here,' Malik murmured.

'No wonder you're eaten up with anxiety,' Lucy said sympathetically. 'Must be awful having to bear the burden of this on your own.'

'I find I'm managing just fine. Believe it or not, in the absence of siblings you tend to develop quite robust coping mechanisms. Moving on...'

'You *are* super self-contained, now that you mention it. Well, I guess when your dad returns home—and return home he will,' Lucy stressed, 'It might be a bit frantic and chaotic.'

Malik said nothing.

'Frantic and chaotic' were not words he would ever have associated with his highly organised, utterly controlled parents and he was sure that, whatever the circumstances at the moment, nothing at all was going to be frantic or chaotic within those palace walls. His mother had broken the news of his father with her usual cool, emotionless restraint and he was under no illusions that things would be in place at the palace for his father's eventual return there for recuperation. A calm, well-run, highly efficient household would be on offer, as it always had been from the day he'd been born.

His parents had had an arranged marriage and he had never spied anything within it that could even be loosely described as 'passion'. Which, he reflected now, mouth tightening, was actually no bad thing. Bitter experience had long taught him that, however stultifying his once-youthful self had found his parents' marriage, it was a damned sight better than the alternatives that lay out there, like steel traps in wait of the unwary.

'I'll naturally make sure that photos of where you'll be staying are emailed to you and you'll be given ample opportunity to approve it. You can trust me on this, Lucy—we won't be under one another's feet. I will retreat to my own quarters when the working day is done, and you'll be free to do whatever you want to do in your spare time. I could have arranged for a PA over there, to spare you the ordeal of this situation, but no PA would be able to get up to speed with all the complex deals in progress that you're currently handling. And also, of course, as you've said, you can't sit in a vacuum for weeks at a stretch.'

'I get it, Malik, but back to the end of the working day situation… How I can build a personal life for myself over there?'

'There's a wealth of very comprehensive tourist blurb on the place. I'll also make sure you're emailed with information on things you might be interested in. Obviously, there might be one or two things you'll simply have to accept as quite different to what you're accustomed to.'

'Name a few.' She relaxed into a smile, mind soothed by what he had said about their living arrangements.

'Pubs: not really many of those, although there are some magnificent hotels with excellent nightlife. Public transport is sparse.' He smiled. 'Your hair might go grey-whilehunting for the nearest Tube. Taxis, however, are cheap and plentiful and, most importantly, air-conditioned. There's the coast and a wealth of museums and galleries and, of course, it's a vibrant hub should you want to fly out to visit any of the surrounding cities or countries. The family jet will be on standby, as will any number of drivers. A fleet of cars is always available for use.'

'A fleet of cars...what luxury.'

Malik remained silent. It would be interesting to see how she dealt with what would await her in his country. She would be exposed to a level of luxury that might come as a shock. How would she react?

He was surprised to feel a certain amount of tension at what could be an unfortunate outcome, but didn't he have experience in that particular area? And wasn't it wise to expect nothing and therefore never court disappointment?

He looked at her in brooding silence but his mind was elsewhere, playing with memories of the woman he had foolishly fancied himself in love with at the tender age of eighteen, when he had been at university in London. She had been as bedazzling as any woman he had ever met in his life before.

He had boarded from the age of thirteen, a tremendous place on the outskirts of Paris where he had learned to speak French fluently. But during those years he had spent all his holidays in Sarastan, where he had become accustomed only to meeting girls from the same social circle as his—girls who had been born knowing their place in the world and the extremely privileged status they enjoyed. Most of them had never strayed beyond the confines of a very rarefied social circle.

Sylvie had defied all those stereotypical images he had grown up with. Slight, and as graceful as a ballerina with green eyes and long red hair, he had met her in his first week and it had been lust at first sight. At the age of eighteen, love and lust had been immediate bedfellows and he hadn't fought any of it. He'd fallen hard for the girl, who'd worked in a hip, vintage record shop. With knowing eyes and raucous laugh, she was a girl with three earrings in each ear and a tiny, interesting tattoo just below her belly button.

She'd known how deep his pockets were. He hadn't tried to conceal his wealth. She had accepted the gifts with open arms and over the course of time had changed from the carefree girl he'd fallen for to a woman who had begun to see the people around her as less than her. She'd learnt arrogance. She'd felt it her right to complain to the people who served her in restaurants. Petulance had kicked in if she didn't get her own way. She'd become demanding.

Maybe those traits had always been there, but Malik had been left bitterly disillusioned, and even more so when, at the end of their disastrous relationship, she had laughed in his face and told him that she'd been fooling around behind his back the entire time.

Maybe she had. Maybe she'd concocted something to hurl at him because he had dumped her.

There was no *maybe* about the fact that he'd been a complete fool. He'd allowed himself to lose control of his emotions and had paid the price. He'd taken lessons with him from that experience. Never again would he trust emotions. They'd let him down once; he wasn't going to risk them letting him down ever again.

Avoiding those pitfalls? Easy. He dated women who were single-minded in their careers and weren't interested in long-term relationships. He'd been honest with each and every one of them from the very start; had told them that, if they were in search of Mr Right, then they should look somewhere else. He'd had fun but he'd decided, somewhere deep inside, that when it came to marriage he would choose as his father had—with his head and not with his heart.

It would be an arranged marriage with a woman who came from the same background as his and would be unimpressed with the magnificent riches that accompanied him. She would understand the value of spreading wealth around those less fortunate who lived in the country, and promoting all those causes that furthered infrastructure in Sarastan, as his parents had over the course of their marriage. With money and power came responsibility.

He wondered whether Lucy would have her head turned by the treasures she would find at the end of the rainbow. When he thought of that, something inside him twisted. Time would tell.

'Actually,' he surfaced to hear her say, dimpled smile

back in place, 'Who needs a fleet of cars? If I had just the one, I would have been in work on time today. No, scratch that—I would still have decided to walk in. Exercise is essential. Although, thinking about it, it *was* a very ambitious walk. So…well… I probably would have arrived at exactly the same time, because I would have ended up trying to grab a Tube train that was never going to show up.'

'Thank you for that wealth of information.' Malik looked at her, still caught up wondering what she would think of what was awaiting her. 'You should get a car. I have no idea how anyone can survive without one.'

'You probably have no idea how anyone could survive without lots of things,' Lucy returned drily. 'A car being the least of those things.'

'Maybe you have a point.'

He smiled slowly. Flustered by that lazy smile, Lucy drew in a sharp, unsteady breath. Sprawling palace or no sprawling palace, she felt a shiver of thrill, excitement and quaking panic all rolled into one. The roof might be huge but they were still going to be living together under it.

Her heart sped up. She would be in 'her own quarters', whatever that meant, but she would still be *aware* of him in the same place as her, within the same palace walls. Hardly the same as when she headed off to her box in Swiss Cottage.

'Are you going to tell me about this interviewing for a bride thing?' she asked quickly.

'I'm not sure I specified an *interview*—and, for the

record, there's nothing much to tell, Lucy. It's something that will most probably happen while I'm out there. An arrangement will be cemented.' He shrugged. 'With my father's health quite possibly permanently compromised, succession becomes more important. It's not crucial at this juncture, but it's desirable.'

'And…does that mean you get married and live out there?'

'It means the future holds what the future holds.'

'And the future holds an arranged marriage…'

'Like I told you,' Malik said patiently, 'This is not something you need to concern yourself with. Your duties over there will be very straightforward.'

'One last question on the subject…'

Malik called for the bill.

She was curious and, considering she was being asked to put up with what might turn out to be quite a bit of upheaval in her life, she deserved to have some of her questions answered.

Knowing her as well as he did, he would have been shocked if she had accepted his offer without an A4 sheet filled with questions. That said, he would have to curtail her curiosity. Her role would be vital on the work front but negligible everywhere else. She would possibly meet his family now and again—it would be downright bizarre if she didn't, given the circumstances—but largely she would be invisible.

When Malik thought of her meeting his formidable, cold and ultra-traditional parents, he drew a blank. *Best not* were the words that sprang to mind.

'Will I be involved in the interviewing procedures? Not that you want to use the term *interviewing*, but I can't think of any other word to use.'

Malik burst out laughing and flashed her a glance as he settled the bill.

'What's so funny?'

Malik opened his mouth to quip that involvement from her would probably result in all interviewees fleeing for the hills in terror, but then he remembered the way she had looked at him with huge, hurt eyes when he had teased her about her penchant for baguettes and thought again.

'You can use whatever word you like,' he said gently. 'And, no, Lucy, your talents won't be called on when it comes to my choosing of a wife. I've never involved you in my personal life and I won't be starting now.'

For a few seconds, their eyes tangled and she was the first to look away.

That'll teach me, she thought.

They worked well together, and they had the easy familiarity of two people who shared a lot of time on a daily basis. He appreciated her talents and, she liked to think, she had a healthy ability to speak her mind without being cowed or awed.

But that was it. Beyond that, all doors were firmly locked and, if she hadn't known it before, he had just made very sure to remind her.

All good; no room for annoying, drifting thoughts. She would have a job to do and she would make sure that it would be a job well done.

CHAPTER THREE

BETWEEN PACKING, PANICKING, texting loads of people and conference-calling her entire family—each of whom had way too much to contribute on her sudden departure—plus sorting out stuff with the flat, Lucy still managed to devour everything she could get hold of on the Internet about Sarastan.

True to his word, Malik had personally emailed her a PDF with facts and figures about his country, and had listed things that she might like to do while she was there. She did a lot of hectic cross-checking and decided that, yes, there would be a lot to do while she was there, which helped eradicate fears about rattling around in a palace like a spare part the second her work duties were done for the day.

She realised that she had managed to omit quite a number of practical questions, but she reckoned she could sort that all out once she reached the place. In the meantime, she spent a busy week tying up all manner of loose ends in the office, and co-ordinating files that needed to be accessible should the need arise for one of the partners, whilst deciding what to pack.

Malik had opened an account for her and deposited a

vast sum of money which he told her was to 'equip herself with suitable clothing'. She had taken that to mean
'suitable clothing' for a very hot country, and hopefully
not suitable clothing designed to ensure she didn't stick
out like a sore thumb. She liked bright colours and felt
that, under hot, sunny skies, bright colours would be just
the ticket. If it turned out that she stood out too much,
then she would revisit her choices.

For the moment…nerves decided to put in a long-
overdue appearance. The novelty of her upcoming adventure had sunk in, as had the guilty pleasure of her
spending spree accompanied by two of her sisters, Alice
and Jess.

She would have been anxious at the airport, with a
wildly different future only a matter of hours away, but
she was distracted by the novelty of flying first class
and luxuriated in a couple of glasses of champagne before promptly nodding off.

It wasn't a long flight. Now, here she was with the
plane descending, and suddenly it was all too real. Her
stomach knotted as she strapped her seat belt, and she
closed her eyes as the plane screeched to a shuddering
stop on the Tarmac.

A driver would be waiting for her. She should exit
the terminal and look for a long, sleek black Bentley.
The journey to where they were staying would take
under an hour. Malik would meet her at the house.
Those were his instructions. He had also given her
the registration number, although he had said Bentleys
were few and far between. In fact, his family owned
all five of them.

Lucy emerged from the uber-modern, crazily clean terminal in record time. Her case looked mournfully inadequate, hobnobbing with far more expensive luggage on the carousel, and she trolleyed it out into blistering early evening heat.

Every piece of literature had said that it was hot, yet nothing quite prepared her for the sauna intensity of the sun beating down on her as she screeched to a stop outside the glass doors and looked around her. The long, wide strip of road outside was lined with palm trees and, beyond the airport bustle, a distant vision of desert brought home to her just how far out of her comfort zone she was going to be here.

Lucy had done some travelling in her life: family holidays to Europe. With so many of them, money had been stretched. They had rented houses in France and been to more camp sites than she could shake a stick at.

But this felt wildly different.

Thankfully, the flowery dress she had chosen to wear for the flight, sticking to her like glue as it was, seemed acceptable. Tourists, pink-faced and sheltering under hats, were climbing into black taxis or else looking around them for their lifts, and there were locals, some in Western clothing, some in traditional robes.

Excitement momentarily displaced nerves until she spotted the Bentley and, as she hurried towards it, pulling both her cases, a driver leapt out of the car to relieve her of them. Her instinct was to launch into polite chatter, but it was clear that he was there to do a job and, after greeting her, he stepped back and spun round to head for the door.

* * *

From behind privacy glass in the splendid luxury of his car, Malik watched Lucy as she tripped behind his driver, head swinging left and right as she did her best to take everything in.

He originally hadn't planned to meet her at the airport. With his father back from hospital, and a million things to do with the various family business concerns which had practically gone into panicked meltdown at his father's sudden health shock, time was in short supply.

The ship had to be steadied. Many thousands depended on the stability of the Al-Rashid family, which was involved in every part of the country's economic infrastructure. His father was an expert when it came to handling the complex network of companies. Malik handled much of the family billions, but from the London hub. Returning to Sarastan, he had quickly realised that there would be a lot of ground to cover to get up to speed with the way the vast machinery of his family's businesses were handled here.

The thorny business of ship-steadying was going to take time. Yet, he had thought about Lucy arriving and had suddenly become restless to see her.

He'd missed her. He'd missed her input. Missed her being his right-hand helper. God knew he'd needed it over here, where rules of engagement weren't quite the same as they were in his well-oiled set-up in London.

He opened the door and vaulted out, leaning against the car as the heat struck him with the force of a sledgehammer.

He smiled. She was wearing a flowing, bright, flowery dress buttoned all the way up. The flowers were huge and in wildly energetic colours and the dress was cinched in at the waist with a matching cloth belt. Lifting his reflective sunglasses to look at her, he absently wondered how it was that he had never noticed quite what an hourglass figure she had.

But, then again, this dress seemed designed to show it off, even though the actual style was really quite modest: below the knee, sleeves, little dainty collar...

The smile turned to a grin. For the first time in a week, he felt some of the tension oozing out of him.

'Lucy,' he drawled as she slowed her pace and looked at him from the opposite side of the car as his driver rushed to open the door for her. 'Good flight? You look hot.'

Lucy hadn't expected him.

Her mind had been drifting this way and that as she'd followed the driver. Her eyes, likewise, had been taking everything in. She'd also been sweltering and idly wondering what would happen if she fainted from the heat.

So she had the shock of her life when Malik stepped out of the car. In the space of a week, she'd somehow managed to forget just how beautiful he was. His raven-black hair was swept back and curled slightly at the collar of his shirt, a white short-sleeved shirt with an almost invisible white embroidered monogram on the front pocket. Maybe it was being out here in the blazing sun for a week, but he seemed a shade more bronzed.

And taller—which she knew was an optical illusion. Baking heat didn't make a person grow a couple of inches. Still, she stopped dead in her tracks and, for a few seconds, her heart slowed, the heat was forgotten and breath caught in her throat.

He had shoved his sunglasses up and was looking at her with lazy amusement.

'What are you doing here, Malik?'

She ducked into the back seat; what bliss…it was *cold*. She closed her eyes for a couple of seconds, then turned to look at him as he followed suit, slamming the door after him.

She breathed him in and felt a little unsteady.

'I wasn't expecting you,' she tacked on a little lamely. 'But, now that you're here, how's your dad doing? It's just brilliant that he's back from hospital, and thanks for filling me in. Hospitals…awful places.'

'You speak from close personal experience?'

'Not at all, but I've seen enough hospital dramas.'

'Which makes perfect sense.'

Hell, he'd missed this. There was a lot to be said for her conversational twists and turns, excellent distraction. Only now did he truly realise just how much stress he'd been under since he'd returned.

'And how is your mother dealing with it? I know you said she's fine, but I'll bet she's not. Probably making sure to keep a stiff upper lip because she doesn't want you to get too worried. My mother is very much like that. My father, come to think of it, not at all. He's excellent at feeling sorry for himself when he's under the weather.'

'It's all under control, Lucy. Best team of medics, best consultant, best after-care.'

'Best of everything—I'm getting the message. But still…there's more to recuperation than the best of everything.'

'Indeed there is,' he replied gravely, dark eyes flicking across her face, still flushed from the heat outside.

His eyes dropped to her mouth, which had a perfect Cupid's bow. And then drifted lower, to the cling of her dress across her full breasts. Something kicked in and his mouth tightened as he quickly looked away from a sight that was suddenly a little too tempting for his own good.

'Sticking to business, however…part of the reason I came here is to fill you in on anything you might want to find out now that you're actually here.'

Lucy would rather have delved into a few more questions about his family. It had been such a huge and presumably traumatic event and she marvelled that he could remain as cool as a cucumber. One of her sisters had broken her leg three years previously and Lucy had been distraught. She paled when she thought of either of her parents going into hospital.

'It's hotter than I expected,' she said, focusing on the guy looking at her with brooding attention.

'It shouldn't be. I sent an encyclopaedia worth of information, including details about the weather.'

'And that was extremely helpful.' She'd tied her hair back into something that should have been a bun, but it had gradually unravelled over the course of the day, and she helped things along now by yanking off the elastic tie and shaking her head.

The car was beautifully cool and her hair wasn't accustomed to being restricted. She failed to notice the sudden tension that rippled through Malik's body as he took in her carefree gesture. Failed to notice the way his eyes narrowed and his nostrils flared before he controlled his expression.

'Questions?' he reminded her, voice terser than intended.

'Here's one. Should I have my hair chopped off? I'm not sure this heat is going to agree with it. English heat is very different to this.'

'Up to you. Not the sort of question I had in mind, however.'

Lucy rested her head back, half-closed her eyes and dimpled at him.

'I know. I was just thinking out loud.'

'Well?'

'Are you happy to be back here?'

'Yet another question I didn't have in mind.'

Lucy half-opened her eyes and looked at him in silence for a few seconds.

She was tempted to probe. He was a very private guy. She knew that: knew it from the way he never, ever gave any hint of a life outside the walls of his very expensive office in London. The place was stuffed with other super-bright, highly ambitious and driven individuals, and yet even these bright and driven men occasionally talked about their partners. Some even went so far as to daringly have a few photos on their desks, which always made her smile.

But Malik was a closed book and now, out here in these circumstances, she realised that he was even more closed a book than she had imagined.

What stirred under that ridiculously gorgeous, utterly impenetrable exterior? she wondered. And not for the first time. Although sitting in this car, with him so close to her, her curiosity felt sharper. Was it because just being here, in the place where he'd been born, opened a door to the background she knew nothing about?

'Questions, questions, questions…' she mused, while her mind threatened to break its leash and run off.

'Focus, Lucy,' Malik said drily. 'You look as though you're a million miles away.'

'It's been a long day,' she said, not untruthfully. 'If I think about practical stuff, Malik, I do have a few questions, as it happens.'

'Spit them out.'

'Eating.'

'Come again?'

'I know my working hours are going to be the same as they are in London, but I'm not going to be heading back on the Tube for dinner in my box.'

'Your box?'

Malik frowned and inclined his head.

'That's where I live. It's a nice enough box. But, now that I'm here, what happens about breakfast and lunch and dinner…?' Her mind played with the alarming thought of sharing those times with him then she told herself that that would actually be the last thing he would want. That dinner he had taken her to before he'd left had been a one-off for purely practical reasons. Making a habit of it wasn't going be on the agenda—thank goodness.

'They'll be provided for.' His voice bordered on bewildered. 'My place isn't in the centre of the city. Of course, I have a suite of rooms there, but where we'll be staying is on the outskirts. You won't be able to stroll in for a baguette every lunchtime.'

'I wouldn't expect there to be baguettes for lunch, Malik.'

'I have staff. They'll be in charge of everything. They take care of everything to do with the palace and personal chefs handle the food. Some work will be done on the premises, of course, and as I've said everything is in place in that regard.'

Outside, the car was eating up the miles. Questions could wait a while. He nodded to the city as they approached it and began giving her some historic information about it. Lucy listened and stared out at a flashing panorama of soaring glass skyscrapers and pavements so clean she could probably have eaten her dinner off them.

'I know a bit about the history of the area,' she said, more to herself than to him, because she was squinting outside into fast-fading light.

'You do?'

'One of my sisters studied history at university, and Sarastan was one of the countries she focused on.'

Silence fell, which Lucy only noticed as they city began disappearing behind them, consumed by vast open space and the darkness of dunes as mysterious as the ocean.

'What does said sister do now?' Malik asked mildly. 'Lecturer?'

'Gosh, no. That's my mum. Jess became a lawyer.' She stifled a yawn. 'I'm beginning to feel the toll all this travel has taken,' she murmured, closing her eyes. 'I'm not accustomed to this. All far too exciting for me.'

'And what about your other sisters?'

'Law, accountancy, medicine… My dad's a doctor.'

Lucy was barely paying attention to what she was saying. Exhaustion was settling over her like a cloud, stifling her thoughts and making her limbs heavy and lazy.

Her sharp consciousness of him next to her was fading under the weight of her own tiredness.

'And you?' Malik asked softly. 'Never tempted by university?'

Lucy's eyes flew open. She straightened and looked at him.

Just like that, the sun seemed to explode into sunset and then disappear into darkness. She was gazing out of the window, and his dark, deep voice was actually quite lulling as he told her about his country. Her body felt slack and the coolness inside the car was making her drowsy.

When he began to explain about his centuries-old culture, it was natural to confide that her sister had mentioned some of it to her on their shopping spree. Jess had been fascinated and envious and had asked her to try and get hold of some souvenirs. She was half-smiling at the memory of the conversation as she chatted to him. But his question shook her right out of her drowsiness. 'Sorry?'

'All your sisters went to university, so why not you? I don't believe you ever told me.'

His dark eyes glittered, and Lucy could feel hot colour creep into her cheeks.

She thought about her broken heart. She thought about the pain of everything that had happened that had made her walk away from the life that had been set in stone for her.

'Well?' Malik prompted. 'Don't tell me it's because you're not as clever as the rest of your family. I know what you're capable of.'

'I don't have to tell you anything, Malik.' Lucy's voice was sharp and cold.

Even in the dark, she could see his astonishment at the sharpness of her voice. It was so uncharacteristic of her. For once, she felt the true gaping differences between them. She might joke but she worked hard. She might challenge him but always within limits, and she was always ready to back away should she, as he sometimes told her, 'go beyond her brief'.

This tone of voice was a first. She had no idea how to break the impasse as the silence stretched between them to breaking point. One thing was for sure—she wasn't going to delve into this slice of her past. Not with him, not with anyone. It was her dark, sad secret and not one to be shared.

Would she ever share it? Maybe one day. Maybe if she found someone she could trust.

'You…you never said…' She cleared her throat and

gathered her scattered wits. 'How does your father feel about returning to…er…work? Is he as much of a workaholic as you are? You, well, you never said…'

For a few seconds, she wondered whether he was going to answer. She could feel his lazy, intent stare burning a hole through her composure. She had to fight the urge to babble on about something and nothing just to put an end to the charge that had suddenly gathered in the space between them.

He did her a favour when he lowered his eyes.

'Nothing has been determined on that front,' he murmured. 'Early days, as you must know, having seen so many hospital dramas. The consultant, the recuperation, the bracing words of advice…you're probably better equipped than I am to predict what's going to happen next.'

The mood suitably lightened, Lucy relaxed and burst out laughing. 'I *am* quite knowledgeable on a range of various situations and their outcomes.' She grinned.

'I'm sure you are.'

They chatted. Questions of a practical nature were temporarily put on hold. However, Malik's antennae were on red-alert: so open, so transparent…a woman with nothing to hide. Or so he had thought.

But he'd hit a nerve and, having hit that nerve, he was suddenly keen to discover more.

This time, when he looked at her from under thoughtful, brooding lashes, his gaze was laser-sharp. She had the body of a siren. A guy would have to be blind not to notice lush curves like the ones she had. Something about that dress had managed to reveal just enough to tease—enough for distant alarm bells to start ringing.

And now...there was a story lurking behind the fact that she'd not been to university. What?

Malik had never indulged in curiosity when it came to women. That was a road that either led to exploring a past they might wish to share in which he had little interest, or to a future about which they might wish to conjecture but in which he had even less interest. He was a guy who preferred the enjoyable business of living in the present when it came to his relationships. Back in that distant time when reason had been lost to insanity, in the first flush of love and lust he'd actually contemplated what a future with Sylvie might look like, fool that he'd been then.

Never again. But now...he wondered.

'There.'

He pointed ahead of them and Lucy blinked at the impressive spectre of a palace slowly materialising in the distance. Darkness had fallen and out here, with the city lights behind them, it was deep and velvety, blanketing everything. The rolling sand dunes were interspersed with patches of trees but, as they drew closer to the palace, those dunes were replaced by carpets of grass, and the palm trees that clustered here and there were planted in rigid lines to form an avenue through which they now drove.

She fell back and stared. When he had told her that he lived in a palace, she had instantly conjured up something reasonably contained with multiple turrets. She could distinctly remember something of the sort in the cartoons she used to watch as a kid: tall and ivory-pale with small windows and lots and lots of turrets, often containing witches.

This was on a different scale altogether. It was illuminated and, against a backdrop of utter darkness, there was something ethereal about the sight. It sprawled, embracing a courtyard in front which was as vast as a park. Pillars and columns dissected a procession of windows, and gracing the centre of the structure was a multiple-domed rotunda. It was a thing of elegance and beauty.

'That's *yours*?'

'It belongs to the Al-Rashid family. I did tell you that there was no risk of us crowding one another. Now you can see how it can be used for accommodation and workspace for a substantial amount of people.'

'It's huge, Malik.'

'Indeed,' he agreed. 'I've never done a room count, but I'd say a minimum of twenty-five bedrooms, excluding various suites. So, yes…substantial.'

'Well, that's an understatement if ever there was one.'

She dragged awe-struck eyes away to look at him. Maybe for the first time she truly appreciated the depth of his wealth and the extreme privilege in which he had been raised. For the first time, she could see why he would consider an arranged marriage to a woman of equally noble standing.

'I get it,' she said quietly.

Leaning against the seat, legs spread, hands resting loosely on his thighs, Malik returned that pensive gaze with a speculative one of his own.

'Tell me what you get.'

'I get why you would want an arranged marriage,' she said slowly. 'All of this…' she gestured to the magnificent, pale spectacle nearing them '…would be too much for anyone ordinary. You would have to marry a woman who was accustomed to it.'

'You think so?' Malik murmured. 'Point of order, I agree with you, but even so…you don't think an *ordinary* woman would be able to cope?'

'I don't think any ordinary woman would want to!' She broke the sudden serious silence with a burst of laughter. 'Personally? Give me a two-up, two-down any day of the week!'

She looked away, just in time to see the imposing front door opened by a man in uniform and from behind him came more of the same.

When her cornflower-blue eyes briefly turned to meet his, they confirmed what she had just said: *no ordinary woman would want this.*

CHAPTER FOUR

MALIK WONDERED...

No ordinary woman would want this? Palaces, wealth beyond most people's wildest dreams, a life in which every need was met and every whim within easy reach... really?

Lucy's amused, heartfelt declaration that she couldn't be less interested in stuff like that, that no ordinary woman would be, had buried in his head like a burr and had been churning around there for the past week, even though no more had been said on the subject.

Instead, he had focused on work, on familiarising Lucy with the layout of where they were staying and on introducing her to a routine with which she felt comfortable. It was up to him to ensure she settled in. He was very much aware that she was here at his request and would probably feel like a fish out of water for the first few days or even weeks.

He thought long and hard about how to ease the temporary transition and decided to stick to a routine similar to the one they had shared in London. They discussed plans for the day over a breakfast brought to them at nine sharp in the conservatory that overlooked the manicured gardens at the back. By then, he had been working for at least two hours, catching up on his own business concerns. As soon as she joined him, they dived into what had to be done that day—it was not unlike discussing plans for the day in his office in London, where she would sit opposite him scrolling through her laptop and quickly taking notes on what had to be packed in.

Twice, they had taken the Bentley to the headquarters in the capital and spent a hectic day there. Things had been well run under his father's eagle-eyed stewardship. Concerns raised about what happened next now that Ali Al-Rashid was recuperating had to be dealt with.

Accustomed to her input, the clever way she communicated with clients, her chattiness and constant upbeat, vocal personality, a suddenly subdued Lucy had taken some getting used to.

'Am I background enough?' she had asked four days ago, on their return from the head office in Sarastan. Then she had smiled and he had wanted to tell her that 'background' was the last thing he wanted her to be— even though here it was exactly what she had to be.

'Perfect,' he had said instead, and she'd smiled a little more.

Then, head tilted, she'd said, 'Well, that's a shame. It's very annoying not being able to chat. I don't think I was ever this quiet even when I had laryngitis four years ago.'

Sitting here now, Malik glanced at his watch and immediately frowned at his lack of focus. His mother was talking. His mind was elsewhere. He was thinking about

Lucy, thinking about how much he missed the free and easy ebullience of her rapport with him.

He was absently wondering how he had managed to become used to a working relationship with Lucy that bore no resemblance to anything he had ever experienced with a woman before. He didn't quite know at what point he'd gone from indulging her enthusiasm for saying exactly what she thought about a thousand random things with long-suffering patience to actually expecting it and finally to enjoying it.

Was it because of the novelty of being in the company of someone who didn't tiptoe around him? Sylvie had been a novelty for him on the romantic front. She had knocked him for six because she had been a curiosity he hadn't been able to resist. After a diet of all the right food, she had represented something sweet and tempting but ultimately bad for him. The relationship had crashed and burned, and he would never go there again, but Lucy...?

This was completely different. She posed no threat to his peace of mind because he wasn't and never would be romantically involved with her. He could appreciate her outspokenness because it was something that he left behind when he shut the office door behind him at the end of play.

Malik was unaccustomed to his mind drifting. He shifted, tried to bring it back to heel and tilted his head to one side as his mother, in her usual perfectly well-mannered, utterly restrained way, updated him on what his father's consultant had said following his visit to the palace earlier.

'Of course,' she was saying, her voice cool and well-modulated, 'Jafna, the senior nurse he has allocated, is in charge of dispensing all the medication. It is a complicated regime, but I am assured, once your father is fully recovered, he will be able to halve the number of tablets he is currently on. We hope for a good outcome by the end of the month.'

He looked at her and marvelled at how rigidly contained she was. Nadia Al-Rashid was a beautiful woman. Her dark hair was now lightly streaked with grey and tied back in an elegant chignon, and every inch of her was impeccably regal, from her finely chiselled features and haughty posture to the elegant, flowing gold-and-blue dress she wore that fell to the floor. She was not quite sixty, but her face was unlined.

She moved on from his father, who was resting upstairs, to Lucy, whom she had yet to meet.

'And this young lady you have brought with you, Malik—tell me what she is like before she arrives. You say she works well alongside you?'

'She knows the ropes,' Malik confirmed wryly. 'She's clever, quick and, as I explained, there's too much happening within my own companies to delegate to an outsider. Hence her presence in Sarastan.'

'I understand. Your father's secretary, Zahra... He has been upset that she will no longer have the job she has enjoyed for over two decades. She was a mature woman in her forties when your father took her on, ten years older than him, and he has much respect for her.'

Malik was startled at this piece of information because he knew next to nothing about the people in his parents lives, far less the ones who worked for his father.

He was also startled by the softening in his mother's voice.

'He can surely shift her to someone else?'

'It is not as easy as that. They have a very special working relationship because her mother was a cherished retainer in our household, and I am afraid Zahra might be too old now for a transfer. Perhaps it is the same with your employee?'

Malik shifted and thought about the shapely body that had made him sit up and take notice ever since she'd come to Sarastan. Maybe that was a little different from his father and Zahra, who was probably well into her sixties if he did the maths.

Yes…definitely a different scenario.

'Perhaps…'

He was about to return to the subject of his father when the door to the sitting room was quietly pushed open and Yusuf entered, who had been with his parents for what felt like a thousand years, bowing, his flowing white robes practically enveloping him. He was small and thin and as loyal an employee as it was possible to be.

Lucy's arrival was announced.

Malik rose to his feet.

She had been here a little over a week and this would be her first meeting with his mother. His father would not be making an appearance; that was fine—one out of two worked.

Out of the corner of his eye, he could see his mother

sit up and prepare herself for the formality of entertaining a stranger.

Under normal circumstances, would she have been alarmed at the thought of them sharing the palace? Probably not. A secretary would pose no problem because, in his mother's eyes, Lucy was so far down the pecking order socially that she wouldn't contemplate her son being attracted to her.

Even more so now, because he had informed both his parents that, in view of changed circumstances, he was willing to wed a suitable bride. It had been one of those rare occasions when he had actually witnessed his mother reveal what was going through her head and he'd been amused at the pleased satisfaction on her face.

He stifled a grin now and wondered whether more genuine emotion might be revealed on her face when she met Lucy who, guaranteed, was probably going to be nothing like any girl she'd met before.

He sat back in the plush, velvet and highly uncomfortably erect chair and waited for his secretary to be shown in.

Standing outside, Lucy adjusted her dress.

She'd spent the past few days doing her best to contain her naturally sunny disposition. She'd met quite a number of the people who worked in various capacities for the sprawling set of Al-Rashid companies.

Actually, for the first time in her life, she'd felt a little tongue tied in Malik's presence. Seeing him in his natural habitat had been…awe-inspiring. Of course, in London, he was the king of the jungle. He walked into a room and people fell silent. His youth was never seen as an impediment. If anything, it enhanced his status as someone formidable and gifted beyond his years. Since she'd been working for him, he had never, to her knowledge, lost money on any deal or misjudged the volatile money markets to his detriment. He issued orders and was obeyed without question.

Here…he walked into a room and people bowed. They were respectful not simply of his talent, business acumen and his crazy intelligence, they were respectful of his inherited status. He was of royal blood and what happened within his vast business concerns affected not just him but everyone in his kingdom.

Likewise, she had found herself taking a step back from being her usual effervescent self. She wasn't awkward around him but she bit her tongue when she got the urge to say something that might get under his skin, even though he'd always laughed when she'd done that. She'd stopped saying whatever popped into her head, no longer safe in the knowledge that she wasn't breaking any unspoken rules. Here, she felt she might be.

He hadn't changed, and yet she felt that she was seeing a different side to him—the side to the man who would marry for duty.

She hadn't asked him anything about the marriage plan and he'd said nothing. Were there women lined up for him? He was following in his parents' footsteps.

As she fussed with her dress, she wondered what his mother would be like. Would she set the benchmark for what a suitable bride for her son might resemble?

In accordance with the nerve-racking dinner that

awaited her, she had done her best to dress for the occasion. The dress was the most formal in her repertoire. It was long, with a pattern of small flowers, and the sleeves, also long, were softly flowing, as was the rest of the dress. Lucy had bought it because, when she did a fast circle in it, she felt wonderfully light, as though she was a butterfly about to spread its wings and flutter away.

Which was a great feeling, because she certainly wasn't anything like a dainty butterfly in appearance. She breathed in deeply as the door was gently pushed open and a bowing Yusuf stepped aside to allow her to go past him.

The magnificent room into which she was shown brought her to an abrupt stop. It was richly decorated in blue and cream and the silk rug that covered most of the floor was absolutely enormous, the size of a football field. The palette of colours that adorned it was dizzyingly beautiful.

Lucy walked slowly inside and, for a few seconds, couldn't resist casting her eyes around her as she admired the tapestry that hung on one of the walls, the vibrant, stylised paintings, the clusters of formal chairs and tables and then, at last…the woman looking at her in silence.

And sitting alongside her… Malik.

This wasn't a Malik she immediately recognised because he was formally dressed in the robes of his country. Loose black-and-gold silk fell to his ankles as he stood. He moved towards her and her heartbeat sped up until she thought her heart would actually jump out of her chest.

Her eyes widened, and they widened even further as he leant into her and whispered devilishly, 'Are you ready for me to make the introductions, Lucy, or should I see if I can find some smelling salts instead? Because you look as though you're about to faint.'

'Very funny.' But her heart was all over the place.

'It's a little grander than where we're currently staying.'

'You could have warned me.' Her eyes skittered beyond him to his mother, who was looking at them both with a guarded, unreadable expression.

She smiled a wavering smile.

'No point.' He straightened but his dark eyes were still amused. 'I very much like the outfit, by the way,' he murmured. 'It makes a change from all those muted colours you've been wearing since you got here. I was beginning to wonder whether the Lucy I've become accustomed to had been replaced with a clone.'

'I *did* bring lots of bright stuff. They're just in my wardrobe waiting for the right moment to make their grand entrance.'

She felt colour steal into her cheeks. The compliment might have been a throwaway one, but it still somehow had the capacity to make her feel all hot and bothered. Upon which she broke away and walked towards the austere and stunningly beautiful woman sitting upright on one of the chairs.

It was a struggle not to falter. Normally an instinctively good judge of character, she had no idea what the

older woman was thinking. Was that cool look conceal-
ing boredom, curiosity, disapproval? Maybe she was
planning dinner menus for the month.

She wanted to glance back to Malik for moral sup-
port but she reminded herself that she was well able to
stand on her own two feet. Her boisterous family had
prepared her to have a voice and to use it without fear.

She also reminded herself that, however terrifying
this beautiful woman was, she was also a woman who
had just recently had to cope with the shock of her husband having a heart attack, and at an age that was still
relatively young.

Her natural warmth and empathy brought a smile to
her face.

'Mother, this is my secretary, Lucy.'

Introductions were made. Lucy thought that 'Nadia'
was a wonderful name. She wondered whether she
should curtsey and decided that there was nothing to
lose.

'Mrs Al-Rashid…or should I address you as something else? Your son never said. In fairness, I didn't get
round to asking. Your Majesty…'

'Nadia will be fine, my dear, and please, there is no
need for you to curtsey.'

'I just want to say how deeply, *deeply* sorry I was to
hear of your husband's heart problems.'

'That is very kind of you to say so. He is, fortunately,
in the best possible hands.'

'Yes, your son told me. How wonderful. It must be
so reassuring to know that you have the very best that
the medical world can offer.' She looked at her host-

ess earnestly whilst still in awe of just how stunningly beautiful she was. 'Sometimes it can all be a little hit and miss, at least in the UK.'

'Hit and miss?'

'Doctors rushed off their feet… Nurses in a tizzy running here, there and everywhere—amazing at what they do, but it's non-stop. I believe—I read.'

'Lucy, perhaps you'd like something to drink?'

Malik's voice from behind brought her sharply back to her feet and she reddened.

'You have a wonderful place here, Mrs… Your Majesty… *Nadia.*'

'Lucy…'

Malik emerged from behind to stand directly in front of her, a looming, six-four, ridiculously good-looking version of his striking mother.

'Why don't you sit? Tea will be served.'

Nadia's lips were twitching, moving to a smile.

'I apologise…er… Nadia…ma'am,' Lucy murmured, shuffling into one of the upright chairs and feeling vaguely mortified at her lack of finesse. 'I tend to talk a little too much when I've nervous.'

'But why are you nervous, my dear?'

'Well…'

'We are very relaxed and hospitable hosts, Ali and I, and of course it is a pleasure to meet the girl of whom my son has spoken so highly.'

'Has he?' Lucy glanced across to Malik from under her lashes and was surprised to find him looking a little off-kilter at the direction of the conversation.

'Well, he really should,' she said tartly. If sharing

space with four sisters and her outspoken parents had done one thing, it was to have taught her that she had a voice and, just so long as she wasn't being mean, cruel or offensive, then it was there to be heard. 'Because without me—' she snapped her fingers, magician-style '—he just wouldn't know what to do when it comes to an awful lot of his deals. It's like that with all of us working behind the scenes.' Lucy dimpled. 'Our bosses don't know it, but we PAs actually are the ones who make the whole place run efficiently.'

Nadia smiled. 'I believe you, my dear.' The dark eyes twinkled. 'And I hope you make sure to tell him that often. Tea?'

Tea was brought and served and Lucy unwound, enjoying this regal woman with the dark eyes that lit up with amusement at some of the things Lucy said to her. Sitting to one side with a dainty cup balancing precariously on his thigh, Malik watched their interaction without giving away a thing on his face.

This man who was so devastatingly handsome in his formal robes, the robes of the man before whom people bowed, sprawled on a chair that was way too small for his towering frame, made her shiver with emotions she couldn't identify. He was the same and yet so incredibly different.

She thought of the easy familiarity they'd shared and in a heartbeat she realised how easy it would be for her to be completely over-awed by this new version of the guy she worked for. Seeing people bowing to her boss, it was hard for her not to slowly fall in line and put him on a pedestal where subservience became the norm.

It would be even easier for him to accept that, she was sure. From everything she had seen, it was what he had grown up with—a life of unimaginable privilege where he was obeyed without fear of dissent. Had he ever had anything happen in his life to shatter that comfortable illusion?

The conversation moved back to Malik's father.

Lucy let her mind drift for a while as she nibbled some of the delicacies that had been brought in for them. They were delicious. She surfaced to a lull in the conversation and immediately filled it with sincere remarks about the nibbles.

'Thank you, Nadia, for inviting me here.' Lucy stood up, taking her cue from Malik. Nadia likewise stood up, as tall and slender as a willow, and Lucy impulsively hugged her.

'I really feel for you,' she confided, drawing back to look up at the older woman, who was smiling at her. 'Your son isn't great when it comes to talking about anything of a personal nature, but I just want to say how pleased I am that your husband is on the path to recovery. You know—and this is just my personal belief...'

She leaned forward, tilting up to look at her hostess and continued earnestly, 'You can sometimes get just scared stiff of small things after you've had a health scare. My aunt had a stroke a few years ago and it took her ages to get back to the things she'd grown fond of doing.'

'Lucy...' Malik tapped his watch. 'Time is moving along...'

'Hush, Malik, and let the child finish what she has begun to say.'

When Lucy looked at her boss, she was surprised at his dumbfounded expression and instantly rueful, feeling that she had maybe gone a step too far without realising it.

Was a hug a little too much? Because she had been excused from curtseying didn't mean that she was at liberty to drop all formalities. She blinked, suddenly skewered with doubt.

'I am afraid I do not quite understand you, my dear. Your aunt?'

Lucy mentally took a deep breath and carried on, because she was who she was, but she was inching ever so slightly back towards the door, conscious that Malik was ready to leave. 'Was very much into mountaineering.'

'Mountaineering?'

She stopped and thought of Aunt Maud, a proud spinster who was fond of preaching about the advantages of nature over men. Lucy had often thought cynically that she was preaching to the converted, after Colin and her broken heart. 'Loved it. She used to say that she was wed to nature because it would endure the test of time so much better than any marriage. She became quite hesitant about climbing after her health scare…'

'Lucy,' Malik said firmly, 'I'm really not convinced my mother is particularly interested in the ins and outs of mountaineering…'

Lucy reddened.

'But, Malik, I am keen to hear the rest of the story.' There was a distinct smile in Nadia's voice.

'But eventually,' Lucy concluded, looking over her shoulder to her brooding boss and saying sweetly to him in a rapid undertone, 'And I'm cutting this story as short as I can, Malik, believe me.

'Aunty Maud came to terms with the fact that life was there for living to the fullest and so she began taking small steps to overcome her fear. Of course, she never really could do the big mountains again, but she still enjoys exploring.'

'I understand what you are saying, Lucy, and of course we all hope that our beloved Ali returns to his duties as soon as possible.' Nadia smiled, a smile that softened the austere lines of her beautiful face. 'Although, as you wisely point out, some of his activities might have to be curtailed. He will tire. I hope, however, that his optimism remains tireless.'

'I would definitely discourage him from thinking about mountaineering.' Lucy grinned and, unexpectedly, Nadia laughed, a light, girlish laugh.

'I will certainly remember your aunt and her curtailed escapades, although Ali and mountains are not a natural mix.'

'Perhaps I can get to meet your husband some time,' Lucy said warmly.

'You certainly will, my child.'

Lucy was quite unaware of Malik's dark eyes resting coolly on her amid the polite farewells as they were ushered to the door. His mother fell back, allowing one of the staff to pull open the front door, and the still warm, humid night air wrapped around them. She'd been apprehensive about what to expect and had been pleasantly surprised, because the very limited picture Malik had painted had been of a couple who were so rigidly traditional that any stray word would have had her escorted to the nearest tower for instant beheading.

As soon as they were in the car, and still basking in the relief of not having made a fool of herself in front of his illustrious parent, Lucy spun to look at Malik with bright eyes.

'She's *nothing* like I thought she was going to be!' She had tugged her hair over one shoulder and was playing with the ends of it.

'What do you mean?'

Malik was leaning back against the seat, legs splayed, his hands resting lightly on his thighs.

What had he expected of this brief social call? He didn't know. Perhaps a cool, polite visit, over before it had begun. As he had expected, tea had been exquisite. He had known that his father wouldn't be making an appearance and his mother, also as expected, had been her usual elegant, coldly beautiful self.

So far, so good.

He'd felt a little sorry for Lucy, landing in this place of well-bred civility, which he supposed would be a family dynamic which was the polar opposite of what she had grown up accustomed to.

He hadn't expected her to throw herself with gusto into their perfunctory visit. He couldn't remember the last time he'd seen his mother laugh and he hadn't seen her so relaxed since… Frankly, it escaped him. Had his father's illness softened her? Or had he just never looked deep enough to someone else behind the sophisticated, distant façade?

Along had come Lucy and drawn something out of his mother that he had never quite managed to get hold of and now Malik frowned, uncomfortable with that thought.

'You told me that your parents were extremely reserved.'

'They are.'

'I suppose when you said *traditional* that I was expecting something else.'

'Where is this conversation going, Lucy?'

'Does it have to go anywhere? I'm just saying how lovely I thought your mother was and not at all as I thought she was going to be. First off, she's really beautiful. I mean *really* beautiful. What does your father look like?'

'My father looks like a man recuperating after major heart surgery.'

'I can tell that your mother's worried sick about him and misses him—something in her eyes whenever she talks about him. But I have to admire her restraint, her poise. I suppose,' she said pensively, staring at Malik but not really seeing him, and definitely missing his frowning disapproval of the conversation, 'That's the sort of thing you would be looking for in this woman you'll be interviewing for the role of wife. I'd really love to meet your dad some time—'

'Enough, Lucy!'

Lucy blinked, focused and then frowned.

'Sorry?'

'I introduced you to my mother as an act of courtesy. You're staying with me at the palace, and of course there

would come a time when it would be appropriate for you
to meet her. That's now been done and dusted.'

'Done and dusted?'

Malik looked at her in brooding silence, lips thinned,
wondering how to steer this conversation away from
choppy waters. At any rate, choppy waters for *him*, because he was unsettled by what was beginning to feel
like an invasion of his privacy.

This didn't happen. No woman had ever been introduced to any family member before and he had never
been tempted to go there. Family introductions fell into
the category of the sort of cosy arrangements that led
to unrealistic expectations of the kind he didn't want.
Whatever ground rules he'd laid down with the women
he'd dated in the past, there had always been some who'd
wanted more than he was ever prepared to give.

Of course, Lucy was in a different category, and
meeting his mother had been a matter of courtesy more
than anything else, but even so…

His reaction was an automatic, ingrained response to
anyone trying to trespass into his private terrain, which
was what this felt like. He reminded himself that Lucy
was Lucy, that her interest was to be expected and that
he had never tried to dampen down her natural exu-
berance or her intellectual curiosity, so why would he
start now?

She would be confused. He'd introduced her to his
mother, so why would he suddenly be tense at her responding to the visit with her usual outspoken candour?

'Of course, you may meet my father in due course.'
He reined in his natural instinct to shut her down and

protect a slice of private life that, he decided, honestly didn't need protecting from a woman who wasn't after anything. 'But, like I said, he's still very frail after his operation. He tires easily and spends much of the day resting. I hear from him in sound bites because it's vital I find out certain things on the business front.'

Sudden silence gathered between them and Malik shifted, annoyed with himself for being short with her, making a mountain out of a molehill.

She wasn't looking at him. She was staring straight ahead, and the angle of her head was proudly defiant, her expression tight-lipped. Something placatory seemed required. That said, it was important that he conveyed the important message that she shouldn't overstep his boundary lines, even inadvertently. That message was more important to him than smoothing ruffled feathers. Ruffled feathers would smooth over perfectly fine in due course.

'Lucy,' he said gently, 'As with my "interviewing a wife", as you insist on calling it, my family life is not a place you will be frequenting. Maybe, in passing, you might meet my father before you go but—'

'I get it.'

She swung round so that she was staring at him. Their eyes tangled and neither looked away.

She *did* get it, and she wanted to shout at him exactly what it was she *got*. She'd been so pleased when they'd left his mother's palace because all her apprehensions about meeting his mother had proved unfounded. It had been a fantastic visit and it had left her wanting more. She'd been greedy to see more of the life that had shaped her charismatic boss and that was a mistake. He'd obviously sensed something behind her effervescent responses and he'd backed off at speed.

Duty visit to meet the mother? Tick.

Any kind of encore? Not on the cards.

He was reminding her of her place in his life: an employee who was paid for doing a job and not someone who should get it into her head that she might be anything more just because she'd met his mother.

The Bentley slowed to circle the enormous courtyard, stopping in front of the magnificent palace.

'Tell me what you get,' Malik murmured. He circled his hand around her arm to stop her leaping out of the car as soon as it stopped and it was as hot as a branding iron. Lucy's thoughts scattered and she breathed in deeply, finding the will power from somewhere to manage a reply.

His touch…scorching her skin and shooting her body down pathways that were confusing and electric.

'I get it that you introduced me to your mother because you felt you had no choice, not really, but that's as far as it goes.' She was breathing heavily, and he hadn't moved his hand, which was making thinking difficult.

Ahead of them, the brightly illuminated palace shone, nestled amid its opulent greenery, the ocean of sand just dark shadows all around.

Malik stared. He could actually hear his own breathing but then fancied that he was imagining it.

Yet he was gripped by something that made the words

still in his throat. He was driven to look at her breasts, heaving as she breathed fast, and had to grit his teeth to resist the urge. Her skin under his fingers was soft and smooth. Her tumbling vanilla-blonde hair tempted his fingers to explore. He released her abruptly and sat back but he knew that he was shaking.

'Spot on,' he said coldly. He raked his fingers through his hair, barely aware of his driver patiently waiting until the order was given for him to open the passenger doors. Malik duly rapped on the privacy glass separating them, and at once the driver leapt out to open Lucy's door.

'Back to the routine tomorrow, Lucy, but I'm glad we understand one another.'

He broke eye contact and pushed open his door to vault outside into the humid air, only taking a couple of seconds to breathe in deep and stamp down the unexpected surge in his libido that had taken a sudden battering ram to his self-control.

CHAPTER FIVE

HE WAS GLAD they understood one another?

Malik Al-Rashid might be a prince, but Lucy truly hoped that he wouldn't think what he had said would be conveniently forgotten. How was it a crime to have shown some interest in his parents? How had that been crossing his precious boundaries?

He'd politely introduced her to his mother and she'd politely given him some feedback. It was the first time she could recall him ever really knocking her back and it hurt. She resolved not to say anything more about it because, on reflection, it wouldn't get anyone anywhere, which didn't mean that she didn't spend the following day simmering.

Several times as she looked at him, reclining in the black leather swivel chair in the huge wing of the palace which had been adapted for use as offices, she had to bite down the temptation to have it out with him.

He was as cool as a cucumber. He'd said his piece and put it behind him, but he'd never reminded her of her status before, and she'd been an idiot to think that, because he never had, then it followed that he never would. It had been enough that she'd known which lines couldn't be crossed at home but, over here, the lines were blurred, she'd crossed them and his harsh reminder had been a slap in the face. Yes, of course he was her boss, and well within his rights to reprimand her for going beyond the brief, but surely they were more than boss and secretary, with all the formality that that implied?

Were they perhaps friends? Or had she got that completely wrong?

Shorn of her customary self-confidence around him, she worked more or less in silence for the duration of the day. She noticed that he didn't say a word about that, didn't once crack any jokes about her being practically mute. He would have done that in London. He would have teased her, coaxed her into telling him what was wrong. He might not have seen that as the strands of a friendship between them, but *she* had, and as the day drew to a close she wondered whether she'd spent years being a fool.

Had that easy familiarity between them just been a manifestation of him humouring her? Had he put up with her idiosyncrasies because she was a talented worker, and putting up with idiosyncrasies had just been him taking the path of least resistance?

Lucy was mortified to think that she'd somehow drifted into the trap of thinking that she occupied a special place in his life. He had his glamorous, clever women, but she had the guy who laughed at stuff she said, who stopped being the forbidding leader of the pack who was so good at intimidating the opposition.

She'd fancied that she'd somehow accessed the man not many people saw. Had that illusion fed the low-level attraction she felt towards him? Because there was no denying that she was attracted to him.

Well, *that* thought didn't exactly fill her with joy and rapture. Yet being near him was like being close to the creamiest chocolate: drool-worthy, but of course off-limits because it was bad for you.

He tempted her, an innocent temptation, and she could acknowledge that she enjoyed that temptation. It made the time she spent at work exciting and she liked that. In a way, she'd become almost addicted to it. Of course, she had lots of friends, and of course she'd dated guys on and off over the years, enjoying their company, but never enough for any of those relationships to develop into anything of significance. She was appalled to think that throughout all those pleasant enough but short-term relationships there had hovered a comparison between those men and her boss.

Ages ago, she had teased her best friend, Helen, that she had a crush on her boss. She knew now that she was guilty of the same weakness, although in Helen's case that crush had turned to love and had ended in a very happy place.

Her crush, if it could even be called that—and the jury was out on that one—was now revealed as a silly bit of nonsense and the guy in question actually thought a lot less of her than she'd imagined.

'You're quiet,' Malik said flatly, just as she'd slammed shut the lid of her laptop and was preparing to return to her quarters.

'Am I?' She tugged her hair over her shoulder and met his questioning dark eyes with a blank expression, and then forced herself to crack a polite smile. The offices where they worked were cold. Very efficient air-conditioning meant that it was vital that she wear a cardigan, and she now shrugged on the patchwork one she had thankfully brought with her.

'Going to tell me, or are we going to have a round-the-houses guessing game?'

'I have a headache,' Lucy told him, reaching down for her laptop and shoving it into the bright-orange vinyl case she'd bought for it.

'Why do you have a headache?'

'I really don't know, Malik. Once I complete my medical degree, maybe I'll work that one out.'

Malik tilted his head to one side and looked at her without saying anything. He'd been sitting behind his desk and now he vaulted upright to perch on the edge of it, where he continued his silent appraisal until she began to feel hot under the collar.

'What?' she eventually muttered under her breath as her heart began to do an annoying drum beat inside her.

She was in a riot of colours—loose yellow trousers and a black-and-white striped tee-shirt, which couldn't help but clash horribly with the patchwork cardigan she had made for herself during a short-lived knitting phase.

He, on the other hand, looked cool, elegant and irritatingly sexy in pale chinos and a white linen shirt which was cuffed to the elbows and hung loosely over the waistband of his trousers.

Why couldn't she stop being *aware* of him? she wondered helplessly? She was fuming at him for his ill-conceived remark the evening before, and yet her disobedient eyes were still drawn to him, as though the pull of his beauty was too compelling.

She was restlessly aware of a powerful urge to paper over her hurt feelings so that things could return to normal between them. It wasn't his fault that she'd seen what they had through different eyes. She'd had her horrendous experience, had had her heart broken and nursed her hurt in silence, but even after that her optimism about people, and love and life in general, had never dimmed.

She'd floated along imagining that, within the parameters of their working relationship, she and Malik had something just a little bit special and she felt that she'd been cruelly disabused of that illusion.

'I'll be heading over to see my father later,' he eventually said. 'I've repeatedly told him that he needs to be on bed rest, and definitely no stress whatsoever, but every day he gets a little stronger and a little more anxious about what's happening with the businesses. I've consulted his specialist who said that, as long as I keep it light and brief, it might be better than to force him into fretful silence. And, like I've said, I need to talk work with him anyway.'

He paused. 'My mother suggested that you come along but I told her that you had other plans. I got the impression that she took to you.'

'Thank her for the invitation,' Lucy said coolly. 'And please make my excuses.'

Of course he wouldn't want her getting too used to the notion that she might be part of his family. She was his secretary. She was the paid help.

'Is that all?' she asked politely and jumped when he slammed his fist on the desk and looked at her with simmering frustration.

'What the hell is going on with you?' he roared, leaping from where he'd been sitting to stride restlessly around the room, hand jerkily raking through his hair. He approached her in ever-diminishing circles until he was towering over her, scowling and as lacking in his usual rigid self-control as she had ever seen him.

'Headache.'

'Yes, and as soon as you get your medical degree you'll diagnose what's causing it and get back to me. Spit it out. You've been in a mood all day and it's really getting on my nerves. You're not a moody person so just tell me what's going on.'

Lucy breathed in deeply. Their eyes tangled and for a second she felt as if she was drowning in the depths of his fathomless dark gaze. She knew that she had to get past this. She couldn't be in a mood with him for the rest of their working lives. She would just have to swallow back any misplaced hurt and pick up where they had left off, but in her heart she knew that she would have to toughen up. She couldn't get hurt every time Malik said something unconsciously thoughtless.

It was disconcerting seeing him in a different light but reacting to it? Allowing him really to get under her skin? That wasn't going to do.

'Honestly, Malik, I really do have a headache.' Frankly, she was on the brink of getting one after this stressful conversation, so no lie there. 'It must be the heat.'

'What heat? This place is as cold as Siberia. We

wouldn't be able to work otherwise. So you can ditch the *overheating* excuse. Talk to me, Lucy. It's not like you to bottle things up.'

'Meaning?'

'Meaning that it's not like you to bottle things up.'

'I'll be fine after I've had a shower and relaxed.'

'Is it the work?'

'What do you mean?'

'Am I working you too hard? It's pretty intense at the moment and especially when we're working here— there isn't the distraction of strolling out to see some shops and get away for an hour. It's something that's crossed my mind more than once, even though I made sure to point out the differences you would find living and working over here. So is it that? Are you beginning to feel constrained?'

'No. I'm not. I knew what I was letting myself in for when I came here. I'm fine catching up on emails and phone calls to my family when I take a lunch break. I don't need round-the-clock entertainment to survive.' She smiled stiffly. 'Maybe I wouldn't be able to do that for ever but, just while we're here, it's not a problem.'

'Come.'

He shifted his gaze and glanced across to the huge windows that overlooked the incongruously pristine green lawns, an oasis of emerald amid the tan of the sand dunes. There was a dark flush on his face when he returned his glance to her startled face.

'I beg your pardon?'

'I said what I had to say yesterday…made things clear

between us…' He flushed darkly. 'But my mother specifically asked for you to come. So, come.'

'It's fine.'

'It's clearly not. I don't believe a word about a fictitious headache and, if it's not the workload and it's not boredom, then it's what I said to you last night.'

'I don't want to talk about that. There's no point. Of course we understand one another. Believe it or not, a little curiosity doesn't add up to me trying to worm myself into your family unit.'

'Why do you have to be so over-imaginative, Lucy? Did I mention anything about you trying to worm your way into my family?'

'I don't need reminding that I work for you. I know I work for you. I know you're my boss and I'm just your secretary.'

'So I'm guessing you were sulking about what I said.'

'You *hurt* me, Malik!'

The silence stretched between them. She was bright red and already regretting the outburst. Chatting about diet fads, her family and her preoccupation with house renovation shows on the telly was quite different from… *this*. Feelings wasn't a topic that had ever arisen between them. The conversation felt raw and dangerous, and her colour heightened.

'I apologise.'

'Do you? Are you really sorry that I was hurt by what you said? You don't want me to meet your father because…because what? Because I might get it into my head that…?'

A quagmire of things that shouldn't be said opened up at her feet and she gulped.

'That what, Lucy?'

'It doesn't matter. I just… I was hurt because you… I suppose you put me in my place and…' Her voice faltered.

'I'll finish what you started saying, shall I?' Malik prompted quietly and Lucy stared at him, licked her lips, and tried and failed to find something to say in response.

'I wouldn't want you to get it into your head that, because you've met my family…'

'I won't.'

'Sure about that?'

'One hundred percent.'

Malik smiled. 'Okay. Good. We'll let that go. Actually, there's another reason why it might not be such a good idea to tag along, at any rate not on a regular basis.'

'Why is that?'

Danger averted.

What if he had come right out and warned her not to fall for him? Not to think that what they had was more than just a great working relationship? Her blood ran cold at the thought of him guessing just how attractive she found him. It ran even colder at the thought of him patiently telling her that meeting his parents wasn't 'meeting the parents', with all the connotations the latter implied.

She would brush past this and find her sunny side if it killed her. She raised her eyebrows and then resumed getting ready to leave, pointlessly straightening one or two things on her desk whilst inching away from him.

'My mother is in the process of arranging my suitable bride. Would you really be interested in joining in that particular conversation?'

'Is she?' Lucy momentarily parked her anger and her hurt, vaguely knowing that she would return to both in due course.

'It's an exciting time for her.'

'Are you being sarcastic?'

'There's some sarcasm there.'

'Is it an exciting time for you as well?'

'It's life. The inevitable arrived a little sooner than expected, but I can handle it.' Malik grinned, eased himself away, stretched and then turned to look at her, hands stuffed in his trouser pockets. 'As for *exciting*... Maybe not quite the adjective I would use on this occasion.'

'I just don't get it,' Lucy confessed, anger and hurt very firmly shoved aside now. 'Okay, maybe I *do* get the whole duty thing—*sort of.* Now that I've met your mother, I can see that life here for you is…a little different than it would be for a normal guy.'

'That's a lot of generalisations you're throwing around. What's abnormal about me?'

But Malik expelled a sigh of contented relief because this was more like it. This was more like the woman he knew—asking questions no one would dare ask and barging past barriers as though they didn't exist. He hated the thought of hurting her, even though he knew that it had been a conversation that had had to be had. Yet those bruised cornflower-blue eyes had cut him to the quick.

Something was going on between them. It was a feeling that came to him as fleeting as quicksilver, leaving before it could take hold. Was that indistinct feeling the *something* that had driven him to be blatant in warning her against getting too wrapped up in a family dynamic that wasn't her concern? Had he been reminding himself of something as much as he had been reminding *her?* At any rate, he was perfectly happy to let things get back to where they belonged now.

He strolled to one of the comfortable leather chairs, part of one of the informal sitting areas in the space. He pushed it back and stretched out his legs to the side, relaxing into the buttery leather, loosely linking his fingers on his stomach and looking at her with brooding interest.

Yes, *much* more like it.

'Where to begin? Seriously, Malik, how can you be so casual about marriage?'

'Because I'm not a romantic person who's on the hunt for fireworks. My approach to life is on a more practical level. Truth is, a woman who understands what comes with being my wife and what doesn't is what I need and what I always expected.'

'Well, you're right. I wouldn't want to get involved in any conversations with your mother or your parents about stuff like that. None of my business and, in fairness, I'm not sure they would welcome my input. Although, maybe knowing that I'm your very efficient secretary, they might ask me to sift through some CVs... weed out the ones I don't find suitable...'

'And who would those poor unfortunates be?'

'That's very egotistic. Some might say that the ones I sifted out would be the lucky escapees.'

'Let's ditch this conversation. It's all academic, at any rate. Tell me how you're going to spend your evening. I know you say that you're perfectly happy with arrangements here, but you could be here for another month, and I'm more than happy to put you in touch with some ex-pat organisations. Might make a change from the four walls of this place.'

'Considerably more than four walls, Malik, and, like I've said, I'm enjoying the novelty of not doing anything at the moment. Life's usually so hectic. It's peaceful just catching up on reading and binge-watching series on my computer.'

Lucy realised that she didn't want him feeling sorry for her. She didn't want him thinking that he had to warn her over getting any ideas about her role in his life, and she didn't want him trying to sort out stuff for her here while he busied himself finding a wife.

What on earth was wrong with her? Why was she suddenly so sensitive around him? What was it she wanted from him that she hadn't before? She been bright and sparky as she'd teased him about his arranged marriage but underneath she'd been edgy.

The question lingered in her head, wispy, intangible and unsettling.

'I honestly don't need you to start feeling sorry for me, Malik.' She laughed off the shortness of her remark but there was a breathlessness there that threatened to reveal that all was not as well as the picture she was desperate to paint.

The dark eyes resting on her were making her all hot and bothered and she wanted to fan herself again. Instead, she began backing towards the door.

She didn't want to find herself floundering in another inexplicable mood, taking things he said to heart because she'd lost her ability to brush them aside with her usual good humour.

'Have a nice evening!' she chirruped, backing away and then, before he could say anything else, she fled.

Having opened the door to the business of a wife, Malik knew that he was on a path that would quickly gather momentum. Lucy had asked him whether he was excited—it was a good question. He'd been honest with her and, as he'd stared into her puzzled, curious blue eyes, it had fleetingly crossed his mind—*what had he done? Was this really where he wanted to go with his life?*

It had been a fleeting thought, almost instantly overruled by the common-sense approach he had adopted over the years. An in-depth conversation had yet to be had but both parents had been relieved that he had initiated the process without having to be pointed in the direction.

'We are both, your mother and I, relieved that you have come to this decision, Malik.' His father had greeted the news some days previously. 'I could die, and an heir is needed to ensure continuity. Too much will rest on your shoulders and, should something happen to you, a lot will be lost. A grandson would hold everything in trust should you no longer be around.'

'Or granddaughter,' Malik had interjected, which had been met with a dubious nod—but a nod was a nod.

Now, here at the table with both his parents, he settled in for the detailed conversation he knew was necessary, even though part of his mind was preoccupied with Lucy and with her moodiness that had made him feel so restless and ill at ease.

An exquisite meal had been served and then cleared. Coffee was up. Both parents allowed a brief silence, and Malik smiled to himself, because he knew that they were preparing what they intended to say.

'I am sorry your lovely secretary could not make it, Malik. Ali...your father...would have enjoyed meeting her.'

Since he hadn't expected this, his eyebrows shot up. He thought of her hurt and killed the sudden appearance of a guilty conscience. He didn't want to talk about Lucy. He didn't want to think of those big, wounded blue eyes.

'Another time,' he said smoothly. 'But, now that we have covered various family issues within the company, shall we discuss what I know must be on both your minds—my impending nuptials?'

'We have some ideas.'

This was more like it. An arranged marriage was simply a business deal and he was excellent when it came to discussing business deals.

'No formal matchmaking,' his mother said, leaning to pour them all some more coffee from the ornate gold-and-sapphire china pot. His father met his eyes and for a second Malik was startled by a flash of amused ca-maraderie which was compounded when his mother smiled at him.

'You are not of our generation, Malik, so we decided that bringing in a formal matchmaker would not be appropriate.'

'I didn't think they existed.'

'You do not live here.' His father actually stifled a grin. 'Some of the ladies would find it quite tricky to find a suitable partner without input from Mrs Bilal. Nadia, would you agree? Not every eligible young woman is a beauty queen.'

Malik burst out laughing as his mother lowered her lashes and tried not to laugh as well.

'Some names…'

'I'll leave it to you,' Malik said.

'But Malik, you cannot simply settle for who we find for you.'

'I trust you.'

'You will not be disappointed. A social gathering… something as befits your station…and, of course, should you not approve of any of the women, then we will not urge you to make a choice.'

Malik's mind was drifting. He would leave it to his mother because she would do a good job. His future was being discussed but it felt unreal, far more unreal than the trajectory of his thoughts, which kept returning to Lucy. But that was to be expected. Marriage to a woman whose face he couldn't conjure *was* going to feel like an out of body experience compared to the reality of the woman sharing his palace, with her outspoken opinions, sharp brain and, now, her somersaulting emotions.

So, a wife to be was a dimly shaped thought easily deferred for the moment. He knew the social pool from which she would be chosen. He didn't know quite what sort of social gathering his mother had in mind, but it would be what it would be.

He returned to a darkened palace a little after eleven. Under normal circumstances, he might have been tempted to work, catch up on what was happening with his own personal business interests scattered across various countries, but his mind refused to settle sufficiently for him to concentrate.

Lying in the silence of his magnificent bedroom, it dawned on him that niggling at the back of his mind was his secretary.

He thought about Lucy and he thought about his parents, and that brief glimpse of two people relaxed with one another, and more *human* than he'd ever noticed previously.

Had Lucy brought out something in his mother, some lightness that hadn't been visible before? Or was Lucy's presence here, in his country, making him see his parents through different eyes?

He would eventually have killed wayward thoughts by flipping open his computer and forcing himself to concentrate but he didn't have to do that. As distractions went, all wayward thoughts were dispelled the second the alarm signal flashed silently on his mobile.

Malik stilled.

He knew exactly where the intruder was. He had the

option of immediately contacting the security team at the palace, who would respond within seconds, but he preferred the other option of confronting whoever had had the temerity to break in.

He slid quietly out of the bed, slung on a pair of drawstring joggers and stealthily made his way downstairs, bare-backed and bare-footed.

It was warm outside. Even in her loose tee-shirt and the cotton shorts she wore to bed, Lucy was still warm.

But it was beautiful. The sky was a black shroud covering everything, pierced with stars that shimmered like tiny jewels. No light pollution out here, and no noise pollution either. London could learn a lesson or two on that front, she thought.

Sitting on one of the rattan chairs, which she rarely used during the day because of the blistering heat, it was impossible not to think of paradise. The dunes were just about visible in the distance.

She hadn't been able to sleep because her mind had been too busy dwelling on how annoyed she still was with Malik, and how hurt she'd been when he'd warned her off getting too cosy with his family. As if she had some kind of hidden agenda! She might have earlier parked those emotions but, once the lights were off, they returned with renewed force.

She'd tiptoed her way through the palace a little after one in morning. It was a massive, bewildering place but she had managed to carve out a few familiar routes for herself. The one she took led down to the kitchens, where she fetched herself some water before heading outside so that she could sit back and let her thoughts wander until they'd covered all the ground they could possibly cover.

The sound behind her was so imperceptible that she was unaware of anyone behind her until she *felt* a presence. Heart beating madly, Lucy simultaneously spun round and shot out of the chair.

'Malik!'

They stared at one another while the silence gathered around them, dense and heavy.

Malik was lost for words.

He stared at her. He couldn't *stop* staring. Her hair was all over the place, a riotous fall of caramel and blonde curls that pelted over her shoulders and down to her waist.

Even in the darkness, he could make out the quiver of her body, which only drew his attention to the swell of her lush breasts against the tee-shirt and the smooth length of shapely legs on show. His libido kicked into gear with painful force. He knew that, if he made the mistake of glancing down at himself, he would see the bulge of his erection distorting the light jersey of his joggers.

'What the hell are you doing out here?' His voice was uneven, sharp, a deflection from what was tearing through his body.

'I didn't realise I had to ask permission to come outside for ten minutes!'

'Got any idea of the time?'

'No! But I can check my phone and tell you!'

'Lucy…it's after one in the morning.'

'I couldn't sleep, Malik—and don't even try to tell me that it's dangerous for me to be out here. I haven't suddenly decided to go walking at midnight in a park in London.'

They stepped towards one another at the same time.

'How did you even know that I was out here?'

'Intruder alarm on my phone.' His erection was so painful he wanted to push it down or else do something else with it. His nostrils flared and he felt heat flare through his roused body. 'I'm alerted if anyone tries to break in…or, in your case, leave. I…' He shook his head, raked his fingers through his hair and shuffled. 'If a door or window is tampered with…opened… Hence I came down to find out what was going on.'

'Dressed like that?' Lucy wished she hadn't mentioned his state of undress because now she was riveted at the sight of his body, the hardness of his chest and the ripple of sinew and muscle in his arms. Her mouth went dry as she stared at the way the light joggers dipped low on his lean hips down to…down to…

Her heart stopped beating and her thoughts dissolved into frantic meltdown.

Was she mistaken? Surely Malik wasn't…*turned on*?

An electric charge roared through her and her body reacted with speed, her breasts swelling and liquid pooling hotly between her legs.

Her eyes flew back to his face but her voice was croaky when she said, 'Well, I'm safe and sound.'

'Why couldn't you sleep?'

'You know why.' She forced herself back in control, told herself that her eyes had been deceiving her. Obviously.

Breathe deep, count to ten and everything will be just fine.

'What I said earlier about... Jesus, tell me that's not still preying on your mind, Lucy.'

'I can't help it, Malik. It was so hurtful. How could you lecture me about not engaging with your family? About making sure I don't go getting any wrong ideas just because you've had no choice but to introduce me to them...her...your mum...? At least it wasn't a double whammy, with me meeting your dad as well and really upsetting the privacy apple cart!'

Lucy felt tears sting the back of her eyes. She wished she hadn't leapt out of the chair because now her legs felt like jelly. She'd said too much, put too much emotion on display. There was a difference between being talkative, challenging and good-natured with Malik and laying into him for something that wasn't his fault just because he'd upset her. But, with her thoughts all over the place, there was no room in her head for common sense.

'I apologised, didn't I? I'm sorry if I offended you.'

'You should know me better. You should *know* that I'm not the sort of person who would read anything... You should *know*...should just *know*...' She turned away but the tears were stinging the back of her eyes.

'You're right,' Malik muttered gruffly. 'I should. Lucy, it was just an instinctive reaction.'

'What's that supposed to mean?'

'I…it's just the way I am. With women…' He shook his head and raked his fingers through his hair, uncomfortable, edgy, yet urgent in his need to wipe her hurt away. 'I'm always upfront with them…and yet many times they read meaning behind something when there's none. It can lead to complications and I've never courted a complicated life.'

'That's different,' Lucy muttered. 'Those women— I'm not them.'

'Yes, it is different, and I'm sorry. I… I've missed you,' he said in a roughened undertone. 'Missed your laughter and your chat.' He moved towards her and brushed the tear from the corner of her eye with his thumb, then he left his hand there, cupping the side of her face.

Her skin was soft and smooth, and her rounded face was exquisitely feminine.

He traced her parted mouth with his finger and her eyes widened. Malik could feel the excited thrum of her body as she stepped towards him and, when he lowered his head to cover her mouth with his, she melted into the kiss, hands curving to the back of his head, tiptoeing to reach up to him.

Her breasts pushed against him and he stifled a groan of pure pleasure. He wanted this so badly, it was a physical ache. He'd never thought that desire could be so painful. He yearned to cup her sexy derriere in his hands; yearned to push beneath the baggy tee-shirt to feel the weight of her braless breasts; longed to strip her naked and take her right here where they stood.

He stepped back, but shakily. He stared down at her, breathing unevenly.

'Lucy…'

She'd leapt back and was now staring back at him in utter horror.

'No!'

'This is my fault.' He took the blame without reservation.

Lucy was in his country and it was up to him to protect her, not give in to some crazy urge to seduce her, even though he felt she had been more than up for the seduction. Looking at her, he could detect the flush of unrequited desire, desire that had temporarily got the better of them both.

'It won't happen again. You're here, in a different country, and probably feeling a little vulnerable…'

In receipt of that lifebelt, Lucy's mouth tightened and she folded her arms.

'Don't be ridiculous,' she refuted angrily. 'Don't you dare think that I'm such a silly, impressionable woman that a little bit of hot weather and a change of scenery is going to somehow make me forget how to behave!' She bristled. 'I *wanted* you to kiss me and I enjoyed kissing you back. It was a mistake, *yes,* but the mistake lies with *both of us.*'

Malik nodded. He should have been surprised but he wasn't because this was Lucy, defiantly proud and honest to a fault.

They understood one another. A mistake had been made and recognised for what it was—a mistake never to be repeated.

He was here to sort out his family affairs and to find himself a suitable bride. Still, he hesitated.

'So, no more mention of this…?'

Lucy nodded and looked away. Her whole body was still on fire.

'Consider it forgotten.'

CHAPTER SIX

'So, Malik, everything is in progress for you to meet some of the young ladies your father and I feel might be suitable choices for you.'

Having agreed to his arranged marriage, now that things were proceeding on that front, Malik couldn't help but think that for someone to have compiled a list of possible women for him to meet in this day and age felt a little weird.

Yet, why should it? No reason; relationships that were fuelled by emotion ran far more of a risk of failure, when he thought about it. He'd had his brush with the emotional stuff and had reverted to what he knew, which was the partnership his parents had, one that had been arranged and had stayed the course.

His family was all very traditional. Marriages had been arranged for the majority of them to the best of his knowledge. He could have gone for the love option. His parents wouldn't have objected. Only *he* knew the reason why he was content to let his head take the lead. And, if it pleased his parents in the process, then that was a bonus, even if it wouldn't have been his primary objective.

'Anyone on the list I might know?'

It was a little past four. Something had changed in the family dynamic and, despite the formality of the conversation, he was more relaxed with both his parents than he could remember being in a long time. Tea had been brought, mint tea served in ornate jade and golden glasses, and he was balancing the glass on his thigh.

'Some, of course. A few attended the same school as you, although they would not have been in the same year. I have also spoken to a few of my own connections with some of our neighbours across the waters and your father and I have discussed possibilities.'

'Possibilities…hmm. Tell me, how was it for you?' He looked at them both. It was an impulsive, random question that suddenly felt important and his father was the first to smile.

'I saw her…' he shot Nadia a sideways look and made a *so-so* gesture with his hand '…and I thought, well, she will do.'

His mother laughed.

'Your father has a very poor memory,' she murmured, catching his gaze. 'I was the one who decided that I might just as well accept what was on offer, even though I knew I might have to get him ship-shape and house-trained.'

'So…,what…? The arranged marriage was…?' Malik was almost shocked.

'It has worked well. That is what I will say.'

Malik fell silent. His remote parents, who had no highs or lows—or so he'd thought.

Was the road he had embarked upon the right one?

He wasn't marrying in haste, but would he repent at leisure?

In the face of sudden doubts, Malik held steady. If he had underestimated the relationship between his parents, then that was his fault. The fact remained that their successful relationship was based on pragmatism, two young people sharing the same goals because they shared the same background. No room for error. It was what he wanted…wasn't it?

'So…what's the procedure for meeting these suitable women?'

He wondered what Lucy was up to. They had agreed their 'pretend we never touched' deal three days ago. Since then, Malik had discovered that some deals were tougher to stick to than others. He'd done deals that had made him a personal fortune but this deal, with no money involved, was crazily difficult to stick to.

She was fine, same as usual, nothing to see there. He'd kept looking. She'd smiled and chatted as she always had. He'd had to fight not to scowl at her continuing good humour. It hadn't really occurred to him previously, but it hit him now that Lucy would doubtless have to precede him back to London, were he to remain in Sarastan to discuss potential nuptials.

'I am arranging a ball. Nothing over the top, but a nice venue for you to circulate and meet whoever you wish to meet without the pressure of anything small and formally arranged. How does that sound to you, Malik?'

'It sounds…fine.'

'Naturally, Lucy, your secretary, would be invited. Perhaps she might wish to help with the arrangements, if that is what she is skilled at doing? We are more than open to suggestions.'

'Lucy?' Malik burst out laughing. 'No. I can't see that. She's more than a secretary, as it happens. She has a brilliant brain, and in fact takes on a lot of complex work more suited to some of my own hedge-fund analysts. She…' He paused, realising that he was going off-piste with his description. He thought of that kiss, and the feel of her lush body pressed against his, and flushed. 'No, I don't see her wanting any input.'

'As soon as arrangements have been made, I will let you know the date, but certainly it will be within the next three weeks at most. And, son…?'

'Yes?' He looked at his strikingly handsome parents, his mother elegant and exquisitely dressed, his father gaunt from his health scare but still a commanding presence. He didn't see the coldness of an arranged marriage. He saw the warmth of two people who cared deeply for one another. How had he missed so much of that?

'Should you wish a different road for yourself…'

'A different road?' His expression cleared and he looked at them thoughtfully. 'No,' he said quietly. 'This is the right road for me. It worked for you both. It will likewise work for me.'

'We are all different, Malik,' his mother said. 'Your experiences have shaped you differently.'

He thought of the other road he had almost taken years ago and then the image of his secretary flashed into his head, confusing him. Emotional, big-hearted, exuberant Lucy… If on one side of the scales there was a suitable wife, then Lucy surely weighed on the opposite side of the scales?

All that emotion… The love and respect he had overlooked in his parents was evidence enough that head would always win over everything else. It would always be the trump card in the deck.

'This is what I want and what's needed,' he told them gently. 'And a ball sounds like an excellent idea. Just let me know that date.'

Lucy was eating in the kitchen when she distantly heard the slam of the front door, a heavy, muffled thud that barely travelled through the vast distance of the palace. She immediately tensed. As far as she'd understood, Malik had gone to his parents and then would be heading out to the city to have dinner with some of his business associates.

The horde of invisible staff had gone for the day and she'd looked forward to having the place to herself, cooking her own food in the kitchen, rather than having exquisite stuff prepared for her, and eating in front of her laptop so that she could catch up on the drama series she was currently binge-watching.

So, when she heard the slam of the front door, she could only hope that Malik would scamper up to his quarters rather than detour via the kitchen.

The kitchen might be the size of a football field but it would still be impossible to miss her at the ten-seater kitchen table, in front of a bowl of pasta with a glass of wine next to her, kitted out in old tracksuit bottoms and a voluminous tee-shirt with a logo of her favourite Disney movie on the front.

Fork hovering mid-air, she watched with a sinking heart as the kitchen door was pushed open and there he was, in all his sinful glory. He was wearing a pair of beige trousers, a black tee-shirt and loafers that would have cost the earth. He hadn't shaved and there was the darkening of stubble on his chin.

She'd spent the past three days with a smile pinned to her face, making very sure that her eyes didn't do anything reckless and disobedient—such as linger on him.

They'd kissed and her world had been turned on its axis but she knew that it was vital that she repositioned her skewered world back where it belonged, on the right trajectory, and carried on as normal.

Nothing had been harder.

'You're here.'

He was mildly surprised as he strolled into the kitchen, headed for the fridge to grab a beer, opened it and then sauntered towards her to inspect what she was eating, before settling in one of the chairs facing her.

'So are you,' Lucy was quick to respond. 'I thought you were going into the city after your parents'. How is your father doing?'

She self-consciously ate the pasta that had been on the way to her mouth before he'd interrupted her, and felt the flick of some wayward spaghetti and tomato sauce on her chin. She delicately wiped it off and proceeded to look at him with something close to accusation.

* * *

'My father is doing fine and, yes, that was the plan,' Malik agreed, drinking straight from the bottle and looking at her at the same time.

He'd breathed a sigh of relief the minute he'd returned from seeing his parents. With decisive plans underway for a marriage he had previously put off thinking about until necessity had brought it to his front door, Malik had suddenly felt hemmed in and constrained. That glimpse of his parents, the depth of their affection, had also thrown him.

A ball... Women he knew, and many he did not, would be at a glittering and impressive event and he would be able to converse with them, perhaps have his curiosity piqued by some of them...or else he would merely attend and assess the suitability of who was there.

He was going to be Prince Charming but without Cinderella, the glass slipper and the midnight cut-off. Something like that would certainly reduce the time spent looking. From a distant memory involving one of his cousins, he could remember an amusing but long-winded situation that had involved a matchmaker and a series of dates which had taken for ever, although in fairness had concluded in a positive result.

One fancy ball, a few dates and his fate would be sealed. The minute he had walked into the kitchen and seen Lucy at the kitchen table, he'd felt more settled. Looking at her was like looking at normality and he couldn't help but enjoy the view.

She was in a weird outfit. The tee-shirt looked as though it belonged to a kid—maybe it was of sentimental value—and the jogging bottoms were faded. But nothing could diminish the startling prettiness of her heart-shaped face and enormous cornflower-blue eyes, not even the fact that she was completely bare of make-up and there was a trace of tomato sauce on her chin.

Memory of that kiss shared surged through him like a sudden shot of potent adrenaline.

He should go.

He drained the bottle, dumped it on the table and remained where he was. The tee-shirt might be baggy, but he could still make out the shape of her breasts, big enough to more than fill his hands.

'That looks good,' he said huskily. 'What you're eating. What is it? I... I actually haven't had anything to eat tonight.'

Lucy tilted her bowl to show him what was left of her meal. 'It's spaghetti with tomato sauce from a bottle and some onions and garlic and cream, Malik. I won't be fronting my own cookery programme with the recipe. Why are you back here, anyway? You haven't said.'

'Any left?'

He stood up, edgy and restless, and peered into an empty saucepan on the cooker. There were two shining silver-and-black range-cookers in the kitchen, built into the marble and granite counter tops. He knew he would find something splendid, hand-prepared and delicious in the fridge. Instead, he helped himself to some water, a block of cheese and some bread, and resumed his place on the chair facing her.

'What have you got up to this evening?'

'You're looking at it.' Lucy half-lifted her laptop.

'You spent the evening on your computer? Tell me you weren't working.'

'Of course I wasn't working, Malik.'

'No need to be defensive.' He looked up from his plate of cheese and bread and grinned. 'But admit it, it's not the first time you've worked after hours.'

'It's impossible to do that here.'

'I'd have thought it was easy without the usual distractions.'

'Usual distractions?'

'Friends, family and pub crawls.'

'*Once.* I've been on a pub crawl *once* and woke up the next morning swearing I'd never do that again. Have *you* ever done something like that? Or is all your outside time taken up with work?'

'Seldom with work,' Malik murmured, and Lucy reddened, struck into immediate silence.

She rose to clear her plate and Malik told her to leave it. It would be taken care of in the morning when his staff arrived. She ignored him and began washing the dishes she had used.

'Some of us had to get on with the business of tidying up after ourselves,' she threw over her shoulder. 'In the absence of anyone around to tidy up after us. In my family there was a strict rota and woe betide anyone who decided to abscond.'

Malik pushed his plate to the side, angled his chair so that he could stretch out his legs and looked at her. Her hair was casually pulled back into a ponytail. Half of it had escaped to curl down her back in feathery tendrils. He could have sat there and watched her like that for ever, and he wondered whether it was because he had just come from having a conversation with his parents about the future that awaited him.

Did the promise of a suitable wife make him suddenly lust for the possibility of an unsuitable lover? Or had he opened a door that should have remained shut but, now that it was opened, continued to tempt him to go inside and discover what lay behind it?

He fidgeted. He could feel the rush of excited blood stiffen him. When she spun round and he noted the bounce of her breasts, he hardened yet further to a point where he was uncomfortable and over-conscious of his erection.

'You still haven't told me why you're back early. If I'd known you were going to show up, I would have...'

'Gone into hiding?'

'Of course not!'

'Then what? Would you rather I hadn't returned?'

'It's your house, Malik. You can come and go as you please.'

'That's not what I asked. You're disappointed to see me here. Scratch that,' he ground out. 'I cancelled the dinner. And it was with two of my father's business associates—an informal meeting to discuss rejigging some of the board members to deal with my father's early retirement. You can leave my plate, Lucy. You might be conditioned to tidy up after yourself, but you're not paid to tidy up after me.' He stood up, took his one plate and cutlery to the sink and, as an afterthought, washed it all and dumped it by the side of the sink, then he turned and perched against the counter to look at her.

'Wasn't in the mood for it after the visit to my parents,' he confessed.

'Should I ask how it went or will you remind me that it's none of my business?'

Once upon a time, she thought with dismay, she wouldn't have hesitated to ask him a question if it had been preying on her mind, but those days were gone, and in their place was this awkwardness...this *awareness*...that no amount of mental stain-remover had quite managed to remove.

She wanted to leave.

She didn't want to leave.

And so she dithered.

Their eyes clashed and she felt her heart pick up pace. Under the tee-shirt, her nipples tightened into stiff, hard bullets jutting against the soft cotton. Between her legs, a dampness was spreading, making her giddy with heat and the burn of desire which she had tried so hard to ignore.

'Have a nightcap with me,' Malik invited huskily. 'I'm in no mood for my own company.'

'And I'm a last resort?' Her voice was breathless, and the teasing jibe fell flat.

'Far from it.'

Lucy hesitated, antenna on full alert, because retreating to the cosy room that overlooked the sprawling back lawns felt intimate—all her imagination, of course. She nodded and offered to make coffee, in a voice that was laced with doubt because the high-tech machine concealed behind one of the doors filled her with mild terror. The chef who prepared their meals was adept at handling it but she feared a mishap if she tried. With this prickly awareness zinging through her, she knew that the wise thing would be to politely decline and leave.

'Maybe a nightcap…'

'A liqueur? There are several available.'

'You choose. I don't know anything about liqueurs.' She watched him as he poured them something amber-coloured in two small, heavy crystal glasses and then, as they made their way out, she decided to give in to her curiosity.

'So…'

'So?' Preceding her, Malik half-turned to look at her with raised eyebrows.

'When you say you weren't in the mood…'

The airy sitting area was a wash of muted colours and silk hangings.

Malik sighed. He rested back against the mint-green sofa, waited until she had sat next to him, eyes alert, and pondered what to say. He reminded himself that this was his destiny and one to which he didn't object. He knew what his goals were and he wasn't a guy who had ever shied away from facing the inevitable. To be born in a certain place, within a certain family, came with expectations, but right now the expectations on his shoulders, the very ones he had volunteered to carry because the time had come, felt…too heavy to bear.

And with Lucy sitting there…with one leg tucked

under her, leaning towards him, blue eyes round and unashamedly curious…

God, it felt as if she embodied a life without complication.

He closed his eyes briefly before opening them to gaze at her in silence. 'My future is hurtling towards me at pace,' he murmured, sipping the liqueur. 'Women have been sourced…plans have been made…the time is coming for me to choose a suitable wife.'

'"Women have been sourced"?' Her heart picked up pace; she felt painful, *hurt.* 'Malik, you make it sound as though you've suddenly been transported back to mediaeval times.'

'Not quite.' He closed his eyes and half-smiled. 'But not a million miles away, at least for me.'

'But you don't have to do anything you don't want to do, surely? You mother strikes me as a very reasonable woman.'

'She is.'

'So why do you have to do something you don't want to do?'

Malik smiled wryly. 'You're mixing me up for someone who allows other people to run his life for him. If I didn't want this arranged marriage, I wouldn't be doing it. I can't remember saying that marriage to a suitable woman was something I didn't want to do, do you?'

'I suppose not…'

'Were you really taken aback to see me?'

'It's your castle. You can come and go as you please.'

'Palace. It's my *palace*…and that's a non-answer.'

'A man's home is his castle. I admit you took me by surprise. I would have… I probably would have…'

'Been hiding away in your rooms? Admit it, I make you uncomfortable.'

'Don't be silly. Of course you don't. Since when have you ever known me to hide away from anything? Since when have I ever been uncomfortable around you? We work perfectly together. *Perfectly.*'

'We did. Until that kiss interrupted the smooth flow of things.'

'We weren't going to bring that up!'

'My apologies.'

'You don't sound very sorry. Malik…'

'Maybe I'm finding out that I'm no good when it comes to make-believe.'

'I don't know what you're talking about—and what has this got to do with you settling down with someone who ticks all the right boxes anyway?'

Danger threaded between them.

The silence stretched. Her mouth remained half-open, on the cusp of saying something, something that refused to be said.

'You're getting married, Malik…' Lucy reminded him jerkily. 'This shouldn't be happening between us!'

'Jesus, you think I don't know that? But… I'm finding it very hard to fight my attraction. The past three days have been torture.' His dark eyes pinned her to the spot, burning with hot intensity. 'Is it just me?'

He didn't move an inch closer to her, and yet Lucy felt his words as forcibly as if he'd reached out and touched her.

'I can't believe you're lost for words, Lucy, but on this occasion I think I like it,' he murmured and the effect was devastating.

She trembled, her eyelids fluttered and the breath caught in her throat.

He was getting married!

To let anything come of this searing desire to sleep with a guy on the cusp of...whatever you wanted to call it...wouldn't do.

But this was different...wasn't it? There was no woman in his life, not even a name or a face, just a possibility. Yes, he would marry, and he would be out of her reach for ever, but right now this man was very much within her reach...

In an instant, Lucy's mind flew ahead and a series of events unravelled at supersonic speed.

A wedded Malik would mean the end of her job, whatever he said. He would surely have to spend a lot more time in Sarastan and how would she fit into that scenario on a long-term basis? There was even a chance that he might emigrate completely because, if he married an aristocrat from there, would she want to up sticks and move to London?

She was facing the end of her career as she knew it, whether that end happened in a week, in a month or in agonisingly slow motion over a period of time.

And then...she would never see this man again.

But she was seeing him *now*, wasn't she?

'Well, of *course* I'm lost for words.' Lucy bristled with vigour. 'This isn't a conversation I was expecting!'

'We could talk about work, if you'd rather?' he sug-

gested unevenly and waited for her to take the bait, to
come to him, to touch like he wanted her to touch.

'It would be a lot safer!'

'Do you want safe? Truthfully? Because, if you do,
then safe is what you'll get.'

'I...'

'This is a time for honesty,' Malik said huskily. 'We're
both adults. We're both free agents at this point in time.
So, do you want...*safe*?'

At this point in time...

'No.'

'I like where this is going...'

Lucy edged towards him and, when their bodies
touched, she hissed a long sigh and shuddered.

She lowered her lashes and the thrill of the unknown
and the highly anticipated rushed through her with tidal
wave ferocity. She could have turned away, held him at
arm's length while she swooned in a suitably helplessly
feminine fashion, but what would be the point?

This was their sweet spot and it was never going to
happen again if she turned her back on it—and why
shouldn't she take charge of her own emotions, her own
responses? She'd been a helpless fool with Colin, had let
romantic thoughts of love turn her misty-eyed and vulnerable, but she knew the score here and, really, hadn't
her background geared her to go after what she wanted?
She wanted *this*.

She could lose herself in a labyrinth of 'shouldn't's...
She could think about risk and consequences. She could
reduce everything to a balancing act, weighing up the
pros and cons coolly and rationally, but this burning

desire she felt wasn't cool and it wasn't rational. It was something overwhelming that needed to be sated and, whatever thought of consequences tried to push through her haze of longing, it didn't stand a chance against the thing inside her, that was telling her that to walk away from this would be a regret she would nurse for ever.

She curled her fingers into his shirt and tugged him towards her, tilted her face to his and unconsciously parted her lips.

'Not here,' Malik said gruffly.

'Malik…'

'Second thoughts?'

'No. Even though it's a terrible idea.' She laughed softly under her breath. 'Although terrible ideas can be fun now and again, I guess. Have you ever had a terrible idea and gone through with it?'

'Tell me you're not about to have a long, meaningful conversation now when I can think of a thousand better things to do that don't involve talking…'

His low, hungry groan was an invitation she couldn't resist but she still yelped and laughed when he stood up, swinging her up with him in one fluid movement and almost knocking over the table with the liqueur glasses in the process.

He carried her swiftly upstairs as though she weighed nothing, which was just excellent for her self-confidence. His dark eyes flicking down to her, glowing with desire, also did the trick with this gloriously handsome guy, she the object of his desire.

And he the object of desire for every red-blooded woman

under the age of ninety on the planet, she thought as heat poured through her.

He occupied a magnificent wing of the palace that was kitted out for the guy who didn't like being too far away from work. She was dimly aware of a sitting area that included a table of boardroom size at one end and a stark arrangement of leather and chrome, so different from the furnishings everywhere else.

When he nudged open the door to one of the bedrooms, *his bedroom,* the breath caught in her throat and she stared around her, absorbing everything as he gently lowered her onto a bed the size of an Olympic swimming pool.

She saw dark colours…deep burgundies, rich velvets, glass, metal and silks….

Then, there was *him*.

She died and went to heaven as she watched him undress very slowly in the shadowy darkness. He stripped off the shirt first and she breathed in deeply at the sight of his muscular torso, the width of his chest, the dark hair shadowing it. She almost couldn't look as he stepped out of his trousers and then hooked his fingers under the waistband of his dark boxers.

'Enjoying the view?' Malik drawled with amusement.

'Very much so.' Her voice was a dry croak. She was sprawled on the bed, watching as he neared her, and then, when he was close enough, he eased off the boxers and she stopped breathing completely. Her eyelids fluttered and she propped herself up on unsteady elbows to shamelessly stare at his impressive, throbbing erection.

'Still okay with the view?' he asked huskily.

'Better than the Empire State Building…' She breathed.

'I'm in favour of that comparison. Your turn now.'

'My turn?'

'I get on the bed and watch you strip down to your birthday suit.'

'Uh…really…?'

Malik leant down, caging her in, and nuzzled the side of her neck and he didn't stand back as he looked at her with serious, dark eyes.

'Are you shy?'

'Reasonably. It's not that unusual.'

'You're beautiful.' He kissed her slowly and tenderly until she was melting from the inside out. 'But you don't have to do anything you don't want to, Lucy. And that includes doing a striptease for me, much as I would enjoy the view.'

He joined her on the bed and undressed her in the semi-darkness, respecting her shyness, and Lucy loved him for that.

She had never felt like this before, never felt such tenderness as the final piece of came off, joining his in a heap on the floor.

She sighed and forgot about thinking altogether as Malik began to explore her body. He kissed her until she wanted to explode, until she was pushing her body hard against his, squirming with her hand behind his neck, caressing and drawing him as close as it was possible for him to be.

It had been a long, long time and never like this. She felt reckless and wanton. She wasn't the young, naïve girl who had once given her heart and her body to a guy

who had ended up hurting her. She was a woman yielding to the sort of passion she had never dreamt possible.
Daringly, she parted her legs so that he could sink between them, and she shivered at the bulge of his erection against her, the promise of penetration filling her
with unbridled excitement.

She arched up as his big hands cupped her breasts
and then shuddered with pure pleasure when he took
one of her stiffened nipples into his mouth to suckle on
it, his tongue darting over the bud, driving her crazy so
that the sighs turned into moans and her body heaved
under his.

'I want you...' She groaned.

'No more than I want you...'

He caressed her breasts, stopping now and again to take
deep, steadying breaths, then he began to work his way
down her body, which was smooth, rounded and soft
under his hands. He raised her heavy breasts and licked
the sensitive skin beneath them... He rubbed her nipples
until they were tough under the pads of his fingers and,
when he trailed his tongue along her rib cage and down
to her belly button, it was unhurriedly, as if he had all
the time in the world.

If his painfully throbbing erection was anything to
go by, then time was definitely *not* on his side. But he
wanted to please this woman, wanted to make sure nothing was rushed, wanted to take her gently and feel her
body and his move as one. Wanted to watch the spread
of a satisfied smile warm her face.

Jesus, he wanted to be *romantic*. It was a notion he

squashed just as soon as it appeared. Romance? No. This wasn't about romance. Romance was alien to him; it was something that was a recipe for disaster.

This was about *desire*. Desire fitted perfectly into his well-oiled world. It was something he could control. Were there risks attached? Fact was, they understood one another, so what would those risks be—what? Besides, at this point, he felt as though he was on a fast-moving train, something thundering along, carrying him on it, something from which, right at this very moment, it would be be impossible to dismount.

He dipped his tongue into her belly button and then went lower and felt her shudder helplessly against him. He nuzzled into the soft down between her thighs and, when he parted the folds of her womanhood, she cried out in a near sob and held her body still for a few seconds.

He flicked the sensitive bud and she tossed and writhed under him. Her fingers were curled into his hair and, yes, he could have brought her to a climax—he could feel her edging inexorably towards one—but he wanted and needed to be inside her.

He was so close to coming himself, as he straightened and hunted briefly for the pack of condoms he kept in his wallet, that he had to try and detach himself—difficult when she was naked on his bed, a vision of absolute perfection.

'Hurry up,' she urged, tossing and looking at him with hot, slumberous eyes.

'A demanding woman. I like it…and I'd like nothing better than to oblige.'

He entered her with a deep, steady thrust, felt her tighten around him, heard her rapid breathing and soft moans and he was filled with a sense of wellbeing and satisfaction.

He watched her as she came, watched the rise of colour flooding her cheeks, her parted mouth and her fluttering lashes, and only then did he allow himself to let go. And, when he did, it was…explosive.

The best thing he'd ever felt, as if he'd gone through a portal and, just for a while, had entered a completely different universe.

He was still on a high when, eventually, his orgasm subsided and he rolled off her and lay flat with one hand over his eyes. He felt her wriggle onto her side and then he could feel her eyes boring into him. He wondered whether regrets might happen. He hoped not.

'So…?'

Malik half-opened his eyes and slid a glance sideways, to look at her warily.

'So…?'

'No point pretending that this never took place.'

'That would be difficult,' Malik agreed.

'In which case we need to talk about it. I know that's probably not your thing, Malik.' Lucy propped herself up on her elbows and pinned him with steady, unflinching blue eyes. 'I can't picture you doing a lot of chat after sex. I might be wrong, granted—am I? Wrong?'

'You know me well…' he murmured in return.

'But this isn't going to go away if we ignore it, so here's what I suggest.'

'Lucy, maybe we could save the post-mortem for

later?' He heaved himself up so their bodies mirrored one another and then he swept some of her long, tangled hair from her face. 'I could think of something a lot more interesting to do right now. Nothing too strenuous, but guaranteed satisfaction nevertheless.'

'That's very tempting, Malik. I really love the thought of guaranteed satisfaction, but I have a much better idea. I think you should maybe go and get us something to drink...tea or coffee or something...and then we can discuss what happens next.'

Post-coital conversation... He had never wandered that road before. He'd not even come close. The minute sex was done and dusted, Malik's thoughts invariably turned to work, at which point he would gently but firmly begin the process of removing himself from whatever bed he happened to be in. He should be irritated and impatient with this unwelcome detour. He wasn't a guy who lay in bed for hours chewing the fat with women he'd just made love to.

'I'll go for the *something* option,' he murmured. 'And don't move a muscle till I'm back.'

He began to slide out of bed but, beforehand, he dropped a kiss on her mouth and then hung around for a couple of seconds longer just because he wanted to taste a little bit more of her...

CHAPTER SEVEN

LUCY HAD FIFTEEN minutes during which she fought her way past hot thoughts of what had happened between them to the more prosaic business of what would happen next between them.

She knew what *she* wanted, and that was for a repeat performance or even several repeat performances. She was still flushed from love-making and her blood was still rushing through her veins while her emotions clamoured for more. Still, she slipped off the bed to retrieve her scattered clothes, which she put back on before sitting on the sofa by the window. Serious conversations were best had fully clothed and this was going to be a serious one. She wasn't about to drift into something unless she was in the control room. She wasn't going to let Malik start thinking that she might be a soft touch who was ready and willing to do whatever he asked.

And she wasn't going to let him ambush her good intentions by touching her, which seemed to scramble her common sense and turn her to mush. Malik was going to marry. He might not love the woman he would marry, but that woman would be wearing his ring on her finger, and when that happened all bets would be off when it came to her own future.

She had already worked out that a career change would be on the cards. That was a bridge she would have to cross when it came and, even if Malik tried to reassure her that it wasn't going to happen, she knew in her heart that it would—as she also knew that she wouldn't try and hang onto to him by her fingernails, until he'd eventually have no option but to prise them off just to get rid of her.

Opening at her feet was a void and gut instinct told her that, if she peered down into that void for too long, she'd go mad. Because the thought of a life without Malik made her heart stop beating…made her want to moan in quiet despair.

It was nothing she couldn't handle. Yet, she had to grit her teeth and stop herself from spiralling. Truth was that the future and whatever it held was obliterated by what was happening right now, because what was happening right now was unstoppable and would be worth whatever consequences she'd have to deal with at a later date. She accepted that, in a part of her that was primitive and all gut instinct.

She was primly upright, hands on her lap, when Malik pushed open the door, with two brandy glasses in his hands.

'You've put your clothes on,' he drawled, briefly pausing to look at her narrowly, head tilted to one side. 'Why have you done that? I want to see you. Please don't tell me that you've decided to become prudish with me. Not after the mind-blowing sex we've just had.'

'The mind-blowing sex we *shouldn't* have just had,' Lucy countered truthfully. 'But now that we have…'

'And there's no point pretending we haven't…'

'Correct. Now that we have…and there's no point pretending that we haven't…well, that's a conversation I don't want to have in bed, because it's not lazy bed chat.'

'Brandy?'

Lucy grimaced but accepted the glass from him. He was in his boxers, and seemed in no hurry to follow her lead and put back on his clothes, but he did join her on the sofa, one hundred percent lean, mean, sizzling temptation.

'What happens next?'

Her eyes strayed to his burnished brown body, the width of his shoulders and the flex of sinew and muscle under the taut, smooth skin—way too delicious for her liking when she wanted to be serious.

And, seriously? Suitable wife on the horizon or no suitable wife on the horizon, Lucy knew that he was a guy who didn't do commitment, and whatever they'd just shared was never going to go anywhere. She didn't know whether his arranged marriage would require fidelity. Would that be part of the contract or would he be able to carry on as normal but with the status quo intact and an heir guaranteed?

She was someone who needed long-term commitment. So how did this fit into the picture? Of course, she knew: he was Fantasy Guy, the object of forbidden desire, and this was her one and only chance to decide whether she took what was temporarily on offer. Because it *was* on offer—she could see it in the flare of desire burning in his eyes as he sipped his brandy and watched her over the rim of the balloon glass.

'What would you like to happen next?' Malik asked softly. 'And, as an aside, have you covered up because you're scared that if you're not we might just end up touching instead of talking?' He grinned.

'Absolutely not.'

'And I absolutely don't believe you. I should tell you that you're just as much of a turn-on with your clothes on as you are with them off.'

'I wish you wouldn't say stuff like that when I'm trying to have this conversation, Malik. It means a lot to me that we have this out.'

'Okay—you win. I don't want you to think that I'm trying to undermine something you take seriously and you're right, of course—we do need to have this conversation even though, from my perspective, the timing could be slightly altered.'

'Malik, neither of us saw this coming. It...' She lifted her shoulders helplessly. 'I really never thought that *these things happen,* at least not in my world, but we're here. I mean, we're here in Sarastan, probably for a few more weeks. Do you know how much longer, actually?'

'Three weeks, give or take.'

'Right, so we're here for three more weeks, and it's going to be very awkward if we start circling around one another.'

'Especially given the fact that we wouldn't be able to keep our hands off one another.'

Lucy went bright-red but had to admit to feeling heady at the flattery.

'So maybe this has been all so sudden and unexpected but maybe, now that it's happened…and I repeat it shouldn't have happened…we could…'

'Let me help you out here, Lucy, because you're going round and round in circles. Okay, maybe it shouldn't have happened. I, personally, beg to differ on that count. We're both adults, and who knows? Maybe there was a simmering attraction between us before we came here but coming here unlocked doors that had been locked before. What do you think of that theory?'

'It's certainly a theory.'

'But, now we're here,' Malik continued smoothly, 'Why not enjoy one another?'

Had he said out loud what she had been thinking? She wanted to have control over the situation. Was this the direction she wanted to explore?

'I don't like the thought of being anybody's temporary plaything.'

'You're not my temporary plaything, Lucy. You're my equal. I don't see you as a toy to be picked up and dropped. I'm not a toddler.'

Would he be picking her up and dropping her? Lucy wondered. Wouldn't she have to put herself in a position of helplessness for that to happen?

She looked at him steadily and what she saw was a guy who was being honest with her. She'd learnt about dishonesty, thanks to Colin. She valued honesty, and this was honesty—raw, unflinching honesty about a relationship that was here and now, to be enjoyed and then released. She'd wanted a serious conversation—

she'd got it. She'd wanted to control the direction of her choices—this was what she was being offered.

'Does this all seem very weird to you?'

'That's what lust is all about. Doesn't always make sense and doesn't always obey what our heads are saying. So, if by that you mean *weird,* then I guess so. But weird can often be wonderful.'

Malik was watching her carefully, eyes trained on her heart-shaped face. Had no man actually ever swept her off her feet? Had she been saving herself for Mr Perfect, just casually dating until someone came along who excited her and shared her dreams about fairy castles and everlasting romance?

He was uncomfortable with the notion that somehow she might start to get the wrong ideas about this new twist in their relationship. Underneath that discomfort, though, was a treacherous satisfaction that he could have roused her in ways no man ever had. He was, however, practical and wary enough to kill that illicit thrill stone-dead. He had hurt her when he'd told her that interacting with his family wasn't going to become part of her life in Sarastan, however much his mother seemed to have taken to her. He didn't want to hurt her again by pointing out pitfalls, but he knew he had to.

'Word of warning, Lucy,' he said gently. 'I wouldn't want you to start thinking that there might be more to this than what's on the table.'

'Meaning?'

'Meaning, as we come together, we will also pull apart. It's just the way it is.'

'That's very poetic, Malik, but I can hear your ego talking.' She looked at him with steely cool. 'Do you honestly think that every woman you go to bed with is going to fall in love with you?'

'Things have a way of happening. God,' he said huskily, 'You're really sexy when you're in dominant mode.'

'You're trying to distract me, Malik.' Lucy blushed.

'I'm driven to honesty. Carry on—I'm listening. Despite the obvious distractions.'

'Malik, I know you're going to marry someone suitable, and in fact this leads me on to something else I want to say. When you get married, you're probably going to end up living here.'

'What makes you say that?'

'Common sense. A girl from here probably isn't going to want to put down roots and start a family so far away from her own family, her friends, everything she's accustomed to.' She paused for breath without allowing any interruption. 'Chances are you might end up splitting your time, at best. In which case, I don't fit in. I'm here on temporary loan to you, Malik, but I have my own life and my own family in England, and I wouldn't be able to hop from one continent to the other as your secretary.'

She drew in a deep breath and powered on. 'So we… we… Yes, we want one another, and it's all about lust and it's going to end, and let that time be when we return to London. Or when *I* return to London. I'll leave and start looking for another job and all I ask is that you give me a good reference.'

'You're giving me a timeline? I have no idea how you've managed to leap to so many conclusions, Lucy. You've married me off and, having married me off, you've now got me house-hunting for somewhere to live here because the woman I marry couldn't possibly have any interest in relocating to London.'

'Even if you *did* decide to return to London to work and live with whoever you've chosen to marry, then it still couldn't work out for us. For me working for you—I would feel awkward and terrible for your wife.'

'Marriages of convenience don't obey the same rules.'

'What does that mean?'

'Romantic attachments assume secondary importance to practical considerations. I give you my parents.' He frowned. 'Although, to be fair, maybe time mellowed what they had into something different. No matter; they would never have been like perhaps your parents were… I'm guessing there was nothing arranged about their marriage…?'

'They fell in love at university. Met on the very first night at the freshers' ball and, five daughters later, they're still together, holding hands and having fun.'

'They're in love,' Malik murmured.

'It does happen, Malik—love and marriage and happy-ever-afters.'

'I'm sure.'

'But not for you.'

'Not for me,' Malik concurred with a shrug. 'I'm not cut from that cloth. You are, however, which is why it's

important that we both accept the limitations of this...
magical thing that's materialised between us.'

He reached out and stroked the side of her face and
then trailed a lazy finger just underneath the neckline
of her tee-shirt.

'Malik, I can't think when you're doing that.' She flicked
at his finger, but half-heartedly, because what more was
there to talk about? She wanted to feel him again, next
to her, under her, on her and in her.

'Good. Thinking can be overrated.'

'We still have things to work through.'

'And we will—scout's honour. Let me undress you.'

She hitched a soft moan as he tugged at her tee-shirt
and then his eyes darkened when she obliged and pulled
it over her head.

'Let's get back into bed,' he coaxed, standing up and
tugging her with a nod to a very tempting bed.

This time Lucy undressed before his lazy, intent, ap-
preciative dark gaze. She didn't rush. By the time she
was lying in blissful abandon on the sheets, she was wet
and ready for him. He parted her legs with his hand and
inserted two fingers into her, slip-sliding them over the
wet crease that sheathed her clitoris.

Naked on the bed, she could see the swelling of his
erection and she nearly passed out when, his fingers
still moving inside her, his dark eyes locked to hers, he
began teasing the throbbing bud of her clitoris.

She dearly wanted to finish what they had been talking about. There was a lot happening in her head and

she wanted to put it all into neat, manageable categories. She'd always loved a list.

Her body had other ideas, though. Her eyelids fluttered and she sank down the bed in little wriggling movements. She pushed her breasts up to him and sighed with pleasure when he began to pay them some attention. *A girl could get dangerously used to this* was the thought that floated in her head as she gave in to physical responses that were a lot more compelling than the intellectual ones she knew she would have to return to.

She discovered that he was absolutely right when he'd said that satisfaction could be guaranteed without penetration—a lot of satisfaction for both of them, as it turned out. She was spent at the end of an hour of sensual exploration, and then was tempted into more than just 'satisfaction guaranteed, no penetration necessary' as she spasmed against his mouth.

She tortured him with feathery kisses everywhere… She took his bigness into her mouth and used her hand and tongue to drive him to the very same place he had taken her. Then, when neither of them could handle the heat any longer, she sensually eased on his contraception, straddled him and felt him swell and release just before she did the same.

She flopped next to him, utterly exhausted, hair everywhere, her body damp with perspiration.

'I feel like I've run a marathon.'

'I've discovered that there are times when it's very rewarding for someone else to take charge. You just proved that.'

* * *

Malik stared deep into her blue eyes in the darkness and something twisted inside him. What was she thinking? She talked the talk but could she really and truly walk the walk? She was deeply emotional and a romantic at heart and, while his head told him that they had both entered into this with their eyes wide open, his heart was struggling to follow suit.

'I don't want to hurt you,' he said gruffly.

Lucy shrugged but there was a sadness in her expression that Malik couldn't quantify.

'It's just that it's…complicated: my life…my choices… You know how it is for me.'

'That's fine.'

'It's far from fine if I hurt you.'

'You should stop banging on about that. You should stop treating me as though I'm breakable, like a piece of china. You could never hurt me. I could only be hurt if I was in love with you, and I'm not in love with you, and I never could be.'

'What do you mean?'

'It doesn't matter, Malik. I should head back to my bedroom. We marathon runners need our beauty sleep.'

'Stay with me tonight.'

He meant it. Never had he issued that invitation to any woman but he meant this. He wanted to share his bed with her for the night; wanted to reach out and feel her soft, sexy body as he slept; wanted to open his eyes to her sweetly pretty face in the morning.

Wanted the sadness on her face to go away.

'Talk to me, Lucy. You were hurt in the past. Talk to me about it…tell me…'

Lucy pulled away to stare up at the ceiling. Her eyes had become accustomed to the darkness and moonlight picked up the dark, circular shapes of the concealed spotlights, the shadow of the enormous tapestry that hung on one wall and the scattering of their clothes on the ground.

Was this where she had ever planned to end up—in bed with a guy because she'd been overcome with lust? Colin had changed the direction of her life and her heart. She had turned her back on anything she felt wasn't safe, and yet Malik couldn't be *more* unsafe.

Still, she wanted this so badly. She thought about her friend Helen, who had felt so protected against falling in love with her boss, and yet she had fallen in love with him. She wasn't going to be the same, was she? She was protected against that because of her past, wasn't she? She'd learned lessons.

That was what she told herself as she continued to stare at the ceiling. She reminded herself that she had volunteered for this. She'd wanted it.

But her thoughts were all of a jumble as the silence lengthened between them until he eventually said, 'I would never want to hurt you. You tell me I can't because there's no love between us, and I get that, but you're lying there and you're hurting all the same. For me, nothing about this feels sordid. It's not a case of picking you up and putting you down. Does this feel sordid for you? Do you feel *used*? For me, what we just shared felt…damn near beautiful, if you want the truth.'

'You're just saying that.' But she turned a little to look at him and her heart lifted a bit. She wanted to smile and nestle close to him. 'And, no, I don't feel used. Not at all.'

'Tell me who hurt you.'

'I never said anyone did. It's just that… I want love and marriage and kids, and all that stuff, and I could never, ever fall for someone who wasn't interested in any of that. Or, rather, someone who might be interested in all that but only if he can oversee the process and control it.'

'Marriage and children… I admit they form part of the plan, but love? No. That's a complication that doesn't feature on the menu.'

'Why not?'

'Maybe,' Malik murmured huskily, 'We all absorb what we've grown up with and a sense of duty and responsibility is what I've absorbed.' He paused. 'And that's why I felt I had to warn you against expecting more than what's on offer. You want love and you deserve it.'

'And it's important I make sure not to stupidly get tempted to look for it in your direction.'

'I'm being honest.'

'You're right. You're honest with me and that's why I can't feel used. We're honest with each other. But you're right about me being hurt in the past.'

Malik stilled and stopped stroking her, all his attention focused on her lovely, subdued yet defiant face up-turned to him.

'Tell me.'

'I've never told anyone this before,' Lucy admitted, but then she added quickly, 'And the only reason I'm telling you is because I want you to realise that I really do mean it when I say that what we have…isn't something I'm going to want more of. That you don't have to start quaking with fear every time we make love because at the back of your mind you wonder whether I'm going to suddenly start trying to cling to you like a limpet.'

Malik grinned wryly. 'Your talent for exaggeration never fails to impress, Lucy.'

'I fell for a guy when I was eighteen and about to go to university. You asked me once how come I was the only one in my family not to go to university. Well, this guy… I thought it was the real thing. I trusted him. When I accidentally became pregnant, it turned out that, for him, what we had was about as real as a three-pound note. He dumped me fast, said he was never into commitment, didn't know what gave me the idea that he was. I miscarried very early on but…it was devastating, Malik.'

She shouldn't have gone down this road because now she could feel tears gathering and beginning to leak out of her eyes and she couldn't control them. She could also feel the gentle touch of his fingers wiping the tears away, which actually made her feel even sorrier for herself.

'Oh, Lucy…'

'I coped.' But her voice wobbled. 'I dumped university and headed out into the big, bad world.'

'And none of your family knew?'

'I couldn't deal with the sympathy fest. They would all have meant well, but it was just something I had to deal with on my own.'

'I get it.'

'Do you? Really?' She sighed, in control now after that shaky patch, although in fairness she still rather liked the feel of his fingers brushing her cheek. 'No matter. Put it this way, I came through the other side. More than that, I realised that Colin had never been the one for me. I also realised that the one for me would always be someone who was into marriage and commitment, and nothing else would do when it came to an investment in my heart. So, you see, what we have here… I'll never want anything more than what it is because I could never invest my feelings in someone who wasn't into returning the favour. If this is all about sex for you, then it's the same for me.'

Malik wanted to hold her close, wrap her up tightly. He also wanted to beat the hell out of the guy who had broken her heart.

And something else was nudging inside him, something unsettling—a feeling of somehow being reduced by what she had said even though what she'd said had been spot on. This was all about the sex. There would be nothing more to come. Because he was that man she'd just described—the one who didn't do commitment, the one who had to oversee the process and control the outcome. He wasn't sure he liked the sound of that guy. That was an uncomfortable thought and one he discarded as fast as it appeared on the horizon.

'Music to my ears,' Malik said huskily, moving to take her in a gesture that was tender and sensual at the same time.

He wondered whether he should try and prise some more details about that guy from her: names, addresses...the lot. Years had gone by but wherever he was now, whatever job he held, he could still find himself paying for the wrong he had done to Lucy. Malik was a powerful guy. Jobs could be terminated with a word in the right ears.

He had hurt her—an eye for an eye and all that stuff.

He gritted his teeth and pushed past those thoughts of vengeance. What was all that about? As she'd said, what they had was about sex, without complications.

'There's something you should know about me as well, Lucy...'

Malik was astonished at the urge to trade confidences, but then why was that so surprising? She deserved to know, didn't she, why he was the man that he was and what had helped to shape him? If she didn't want him thinking that she might cling, then why would he not want her to realise why her clinging would never work? With all the facts on the table, there would be no room for misunderstandings, because she was right—the time left to them was limited. He would marry and, yes, at least to start with he would end up splitting time between Sarastan and London until everything was settled: until his new wife found her feet within the marriage sufficiently to commit to living in London full-time, always with the expectation of returning to Sarastan to live.

There was no point dodging what was probably inevitable. Also…being lumped into the same box as a commitment-phobic, lying snake of an ex who had strung her along and hurt her made Malik's teeth grind together with impotent fury. It was an insult!

'What?' She smiled. 'You don't have to tell me anything you don't want to. I know you for who you are—no surprises in store for me. I know the man I'm dealing with. You don't have to warn me off you.'

She stroked his tough, hard body, skimming her hand over his chest, but he stilled her hand.

'In a minute.'

'Sex *in a minute*? Should I diarise that, Malik? You're the guy who's all about the sex. Right here and right now, no promises made, no questions asked.'

'Now you're making me sound shallow.'

'If the cap fits…'

'I've had my own share of crap,' he confessed gruffly. 'Not on a par with you, but I too met a woman who let me down, a woman who wasn't what she claimed to be. I met her when I was the same age as you were when you got your heart broken by that creep.' She was staring at him with her wide, cornflower-blue eyes and her mouth half-open. He should have felt uncomfortable breaking habits of a lifetime and telling her something he'd never told a soul but he didn't. He felt a sense of release.

'She hurt you.'

'She hurt my pride,' Malik corrected grimly. 'It was enough for me to realise that what my parents had was foolproof—no room for anyone getting hurt, and I'm not talking about myself. I'm talking about a woman getting into a relationship with me and wanting more than

I feel capable of giving because, after Sylvie, there's no room in me for love and fairy tales—not that, looking back, love was part of what I felt for the woman. May have seemed so at the time, but in the final reckoning I believe it's an emotion that's alien to me.

'Like I said to you, we all bounce right back to what we've been exposed to. In your case, heartbreak didn't make you turn your back on love, because you look to your parents and want what they have. It just narrowed the pursuit. And for me? No broken heart but an experience that made me look over my shoulder to my parents' arranged marriage and admire it for what it was—and even more so now because I suspect, after all this time, that despite the practical nature of their marriage they opened a door to affection and possibly even love.'

'I'm really sorry, Malik. Sylvie…what a pretty name. Was she very beautiful? I'm imagining long, straight hair, big green eyes and an elfin figure…'

'This touchy-feely stuff really isn't me, and whether she was beautiful or not with an elfin figure is by the by,' Malik drawled in response, but there was a reluctant grin on his mouth. 'But it seemed fair to put all the cards on the table because…'

'You don't have to spell it out. I know why you told me, and it was more than just putting those cards on the table, wasn't it?'

'Life, for me, is in a state of flux and I would never ask you to put yourself out to accommodate me. Like you said, you have friends and family and a social life in England.'

'So you really think you'll end up living here?'

'I have no idea what that particular slice of the future holds for me, but you raised a good point when you said that there might be a need for anyone I marry to at least have a period of adjustment before heading to London to put down roots. However well-travelled and cosmopolitan a woman might be, there's a difference between seeing the world and settling down to live in a part of it you've never lived in before.'

'And while we both have this time together…'

'We can both accept that there's nothing beyond what we enjoy in the here and now and we both have our reasons. We understand one another. You wanted to reassure me that you weren't going to want more than I could give, and I wanted to let you know why there would be nothing more than what's on the table.' He paused. 'And what's on the table will be…spectacular.'

'Spectacular…'

'I'll leave you with memories to last a lifetime.'

Something uneasy feathered Lucy's spine but she brushed that aside, because the slate was clean, and what lay ahead would be pure, carnal bliss…and she wanted that so badly, it hurt. Desire was powerful enough to stampede every niggling obstacle that lay in its way. They both knew the ropes; lines had been drawn. This would work, this freedom to taste, sample and enjoy one another without guilt or regret, a chapter closed once their time was up.

She wound her arms around him and drew him close enough to feel his heart beating in tune with hers.

'Well, we might as well start with the memory box now, don't you think?'

'Oh, yes…' Malik growled. 'I very much *think*…'

CHAPTER EIGHT

MALIK GLANCED AT LUCY, who was staring out of the window of the four-by-four with a rapt expression.

'What's going through your head?'

Lucy dragged her attention away from the rolling sand dunes surrounding them. The sky was ablaze with the vibrant colours of twilight: oranges, indigos and silver. In half an hour, all those colours would be consumed by the sort of blackness she was only now becoming accustomed to.

Half an hour before, as Malik had driven away from the city and its outskirts into uninhabited terrain, she had glimpsed a group of camels lounging around under the shade of a clump of sparse, oddly shaped trees.

'I'm thinking that this is a one-off for me. Honestly, five days at an all-inclusive in Tenerife pales in comparison.'

'Was that your last holiday?'

'Last family holiday that we all took together? That was a couple of years ago. Rose was tying the knot and we wanted to do something together one last time. Do you remember I told you all about it afterwards?'

'How could I forget the bridesmaid falling in the

fountain?' Malik quipped drily. 'Not to mention the pink dress with the frills you said you were made to wear against your better judgement but then ended up loving it when you saw the photos afterwards. Wasn't there also a last-minute panic about the weather…which turned out all right because the sun shone at all the right times?'

'You have an incredible memory, Malik.'

'So it would seem.' He slid a dark glance across to her and then tore them away with difficulty to focus on the hazardous road winding through the dunes.

'To be fair, I talk quite a bit, so it'd be impossible not to pick things up along the way. But, yes, that was the last big family thing.'

'Busy.'

'Like you wouldn't believe. When most parents were finding out that their adult kids don't fancy going on holiday with them, my parents were making hectic plans so that we could all be together. In fairness, they're always fantastic fun. We all contribute according to what we can afford and then pull straws to find out who's sharing a room with who.'

'Sounds like a nightmare.'

'Slow down, Malik! I can just about spot some more camels over there!'

She tapped him reprovingly on the arm. Malik half-smiled at the absent-minded gesture and obeyed.

Things had changed between them and it wasn't just because they were now lovers. Since he and Lucy had climbed into bed, free to enjoy one another in the most perfect, no-strings-attached situation he could ever have dreamt possible, everyone and everything that had been in the way of him touching her had been hard to bear.

Three days of having to go into the office to oversee complex transference of duties between various CEOs had been a pain. Looking at her as she'd dutifully done her job, head down, ignoring him, had made him fidget with impatience. He had found himself glancing at his watch even more than usual on his visits to his parents, counting the seconds until he could get back to his palace and bury himself in her body. He'd sit there, barely taking in things his mother was saying, surfacing only when it was time to go.

Right now, Lucy was waxing lyrical about camels.

'Have you ever ridden one?' she was asking.

Malik could feel her eager blue eyes on him. 'When you grow up with desert all around, it ends up being inevitable.' He smiled and glanced at her, wanting to let that glance linger, but the driving conditions were too hostile for that indulgence.

'Very exciting.'

'And occasionally smelly.'

She laughed and his smile widened. He enjoyed the sound of her laugh. Out of the blue, he wondered whether this was normal. Was it? Was it normal to miss someone the way he missed her whenever she happened to be somewhere else? Was it normal to think about *her*— not always think about the great sex they shared but instead to think about the pleasure of hearing her laugh?

Was he missing a trick here? Should alarm bells be sounding? No, surely not? She was as relaxed as he was, and no mention was ever made of when things would end between them. They were both living in the moment and of course there was nothing disturbing about that. He was accustomed to laying down ground rules with the women he dated. It was his comfort zone.

He decided that there was no cause for unease in this situation. Plans for the upcoming ball were moving quickly ahead. Malik knew that it was a subject he would have to raise with Lucy pretty soon but the back burner, for the moment, seemed a pretty good place on which to park those good intentions.

It was much more satisfying listening to her chat about this, that and nothing in particular while eagerly drinking in all the sights he showed her.

Such as right now: twilight, camels and sand dunes; what better? And she had no idea where he was taking her, so she was in for a pleasant surprise, and he couldn't wait to see her face when they got there.

'You still haven't told me where we're going.'

'I want to surprise you.'

'Who says you haven't done that already?'

'Have I?' There was a wicked smile in his voice. 'How? No…don't tell me. I can guess. Your body tells me how much I surprise you every time I touch it.'

'There's more to life than pleasant surprises between the sheets.'

Malik burst out laughing.

'You're right and we're heading to one of them right now. Look ahead—see those lights in the distance?'

Lucy followed his hand as the four-by-four gently contoured the dunes to approach the lights. They looked like stars twinkling against the black velvet of the night. Actually her mind was only half on the approaching sight which, as they got nearer, she realised was an elaborate set-up: a billowing tent, a small building and people busily tending to food, a table with white starched linen set for two.

An extravagant dining experience for the two of them. She should be fizzing with excitement but, somewhere inside, she felt flat. When she had told him how much he surprised her, she hadn't been talking about the fantastic things he did to her body, the wonderful way he had of making it come to life under his skilful touch.

No, she had been talking about small stuff. He surprised her in the little confidences he shared without realising, such as when he'd told her about going to see the headmaster at his uber-expensive boarding school because one of his friends had been so desperately homesick Malik had been worried about his mental health. Or when he'd said wistfully that he'd always wanted a dog, but that had been comprehensively banned. Or the way he had of always making sure she was okay, always slowing down to accommodate her so that he never, ever strode ahead. In a thousand ways, he was so much more the man she had only ever glimpsed during office hours.

Her heartbeat quickened. She'd gone into this with her eyes wide open, knowing what she wanted and needed from it, and determined not to let the past determine the present.

But, now, she was in deep. One minute she'd been happily paddling around in the shallow end, the next minute she couldn't see the bottom of the pool and, when she looked over her shoulder, there was nowhere safe to head to. The sides of the pool had disappeared, and she was floundering in an ocean of disaster. She'd fallen for this guy and just admitting it to herself made her whole body tingle with suffocating panic.

She was barely aware of the car rounding to a stop or the door being held open for her by one of the many staff there who were all dressed in identical white robes and sandals.

Malik joined her, neatly hooking her hand into the crook of his arm. 'Tonight you're going to be treated to the finest cuisine my country can offer, prepared and cooked by one of the top chefs in the kingdom.'

'Dining under the stars,' Lucy said, dutifully impressed, 'I hope they won't mind me taking a thousand pictures to send to my family. This is just the sort of thing they'd love.'

When had that happened and what was she going to do now?

'Sit. Tonight is your night and I want you to savour every second of it.'

She was wearing a light pashmina over her dress and Malik scooped it off her and handed it to someone who appeared from nowhere to relieve him of it. Despite the number of people all there to make this evening memorable, it still felt incredibly private and intimate.

Lucy was frantically thinking while she rustled up a smile and gazed around her appreciatively. *Okay, we're here and there's no going back. The main thing is...keep your feelings to yourself.* They'd laid their respective cards on the table and no way was she going to suddenly kid herself into thinking that anything more would come of this than what he'd said from the start.

'You're the first person I've ever done this with,' Malik confided.

'That's a shame. It's so beautiful out here. If I could think of anywhere comparable, then I'd say, but I honestly can't. In fairness, as you know, I don't have much credit in my holiday destination account. A few places in Europe, and here and there in England and Wales— nothing like this. The only sand I've ever experienced has been on a beach filled with people getting lobster-red.'

She loved him and she wanted him and, short of making up some excuse to leave the country, she was here for another couple of weeks. She'd always known that it wasn't going to last. She'd set the deadline herself!

'Can I say something?'

'Sure.'

Plates of nibbles were brought to them, along with iced water and iced champagne in a silver bucket. The cork popped, the bubbles fizzed and she took a sip and looked at Malik over the rim of her glass.

He was devastatingly handsome, in a white shirt and grey linen trousers. She tingled when she looked at him, couldn't bear to tear her eyes away.

'When you return to London, I think you should consider going to university.'

'Huh?'

'You've explained why you didn't go all those years ago and, when I think about that, I see red. But that was then. Now, you could climb any ladder you wanted with the right ducks in a row.'

'You mean a ladder up the money tree?'

'Nothing wrong with that.'

'Not really who I am,' Lucy said truthfully.

God, he was so beautiful. Her heart was already breaking but at the same time she was already deciding that a broken heart now was going to be the same as a broken heart in a couple of weeks' time, so why not enjoy what she had? Why not live in this moment and feast on what was on offer instead of trying to find ways to make a martyr of herself?

She relaxed. It was under-cover love… But, while she remained here, yes, she would have her fill of this beautiful man.

'Can I hold your hand?' she whispered, and looked furtively over her shoulder. 'Or is that kind of thing out of bounds for VIPs like you?'

'Of course you can,' Malik said gently.

'Good.' She briefly linked her fingers with his and squeezed his hand. 'Great nibbles, by the way. Honestly, I'm going to return to London a thousand pounds heavier than when I came here.' She thought that reminding herself frequently about London and returning to it would be a good idea, would keep things a little in perspective and would stop her daydreaming about stuff that was never going to happen.

'Promise me you'll never go on a diet,' Malik said seriously. 'I like your curves.' He shot her a wolfish smile that made her go hot with a sudden urge to hold more than his hand.

'I'll have to see how that stacks up with the hunk waiting to meet me in a few months' time.'

'What hunk?'

'Haven't found him yet,' Lucy said airily, mentally crossing her fingers at the lie. 'But the search will definitely be on when I get back to cold, wet London. Maybe I'll set one of my sisters on it. They all fancy themselves as matchmakers.'

'Doesn't do to rush into anything.'

Lucy looked at him with an amused expression whilst thinking that *that* was rich coming from the guy who was about to rush into marriage with a woman he didn't know from Adam.

'I'm not getting any younger! Last thing I want is to end up playing Fun Aunty at the age of sixty to a thousand nephews and nieces.'

'I'm going to miss your talent for exaggeration.'

Then hold on to me!

Lucy killed that treacherous thought and sat back as more food was brought and glasses were refilled.

'I could help you.'

'Sorry?'

'You say you're not interested in money but who doesn't want to make the most of their potential? And you've got bags of that, Lucy. I would be honoured to fund you for whatever it costs for you to get back into the maths degree you walked away from. That could be returning to university or, more than that, I could easily sponsor you to work in a company while you do it so that you earn as you go with a guarantee of a brilliant job afterwards. What do you say?'

Lucy stuck one hand on her lap, balled it into a fist and focused on the food in front of her while she fought off a tidal wave of hurt. He meant well, and that was the worst of it. He wasn't going to be happy having her leave, but he'd already resigned himself to it, and was now wiping his conscience clean of any unwelcome post-affair stains by lending her a helping hand financially.

'What a tempting offer, Malik. I actually haven't given much thought to what I'll do once I get back to London, but once I leave here I don't think we should have any sort of continuing arrangement with one another.'

'Continuing arrangement?'

'You sponsor me to do something I'm not interested in doing... I keep in touch to fill you in on how it's going because you're the paymaster... You give me pep talks now and again... No; clean break when I leave.'

Malik flushed darkly. 'I would never want anything back from you. I would never consider myself your "paymaster".'

'I'm sorry. That was unfair of me. I guess all I'm saying is I don't think applying for a university place is going to be on the agenda.'

'Can I at least ask why?'

Lucy sighed. 'Those days have come and gone. I'm not bothered by getting a degree. I should be able to get by just fine with a good reference from you and my own ability to work hard. Remind me why we're wasting time talking about this?' She tried a wolfish smile of her own, but wasn't sure she quite managed to pull it off, because he certainly wasn't looking like a guy on the brink of dragging her off to the nearest secluded spot so that he could have his deliciously wicked way with her.

'Because it's something that needs to be discussed.'

'Why?'

She watched, eyebrows raised, as he raked his fingers through his hair and scowled.

'This isn't about lots of chat.' She purred, giving him a taste of his own medicine and taking perverse pleasure in it. 'This is about other, more interesting things...' She sat back and looked around her. 'Like me enjoying this incredible scenery because I probably will never set eyes on it again...and tasting every morsel of this food, even if it turns me into a beached whale after I've eaten the lot... And of course, when we get back to the bedroom, well...'

'Forgive me for trying to do what's good for you,' Malik responded tersely.

'Don't you worry your head about what happens to me when I leave Sarastan. What's good for me is for us to just have some fun with what time we have left.' There was enough sincerity in that remark for her voice to husk over with genuine emotion, and in return Malik sighed and shook his head, as though fighting against the need to dismiss a conversation he wanted to have.

She was stuffed by the end of the evening. They had enjoyed an array of starters, letting the darkness soak them up, and appreciating the studded starry sky above. For the various desserts and coffee, they retired under an elaborate tent that was complete with all mod cons.

Lucy was beginning to feel tired. It had been a long day, and there was something a little exhausting about being presented with spectacular sights, one on top the other, from the wide-open dunes to the roaring twilight, from the camels and the emptiness to the wonderful finale he had arranged for her. Everything felt like a memory in the making and, as they slowly drifted back to the car, which was to be driven back for them, she suddenly had to know how much time was left to them.

She was determined to enjoy what was left, determined not to let their last few moments be blighted by anxiety and trepidation about a future without him. She wanted to be in charge of her own narrative. Wasn't it a fact that the only stuff you ever regretted was the stuff you wanted to do but never did? She had embarked on this crazy, whirlwind, beautiful, invigorating affair because she would have regretted having walked away from it.

She wasn't going to regret a single minute of what they had shared, even if it left her with a broken heart. There was something to be said for that old chestnut about it being better to have loved and lost than never to have loved at all. Which wasn't to say that a little mental preparation for departure wasn't going to be in order.

'So...'

'I'm beginning to dread when you open a sentence with *so*...'

Lucy ignored the interruption. It was good that Malik wasn't doing the driving. She had his full attention.

'We've had our chat,' she said, 'About what happens once I return to London—and many thanks, incidentally, for the kind offer of giving me a leg up the career ladder.'

'You should seriously think about it. A maths degree could open a lot more doors for you.'

'Like I said, I'm perfectly happy living with those doors shut. But what I'd really like to know now is when I can start planning my return. I want to make sure everything is okay with my place for when I get back. I can arrange for one of my sisters to nip in and have a look and make sure that the fridge is stocked for when I get in.'

'You need notice to get someone to buy some milk for when you return?'

'It's not a joke, Malik. I might want to start arranging interviews for when I'm back in London, and I can't do that if I have no idea when that's going to be, can I?'

'There's really no need for you to start job-hunting immediately,' Malik ground out with a sudden, darkening frown. 'I'm not rushing you out of the door.'

'I know you're not,' Lucy returned equably. 'I know you'd never do that, but I don't see any value in hanging around with nothing much to do once I'm back in London. It's just not in my nature.'

'We really don't have to have this conversation at the moment. Do we?'

'I can't believe you're saying that, Malik,' Lucy said with a wry smile, 'When you're the guy who's said more than once that only fools put off for tomorrow what has to be done today.'

'Remind me to avoid sharing pearls of wisdom with you from now on,' he drawled, lounging against the seat and looking so sinfully sexy that Lucy was very tempted to do just as asked and ditch the uncomfortable conversation in favour of shamelessly staring at him.

'I won't be around for you to share them with,' she returned more sharply than she'd intended. 'So...'

'A week and a half, if I'm forced to put a timeline on it. As you know, the brunt of the work transferring responsibility to various other people within the company has gone better than expected, and thankfully my father has agreed to return on a limited basis because his recovery is going well, so any remaining transfers of duty can be handled by him.'

'Less time than I thought. Fair enough.' She breathed in thinly and forced a smile. 'Maybe your father thinks that he might end up bored stiff if he decides to stay at home, pruning the roses and playing golf.'

Malik burst out laughing and looked at her with warm, dark appreciation.

She was flushed and her blonde hair curled over her shoulders, a tangle of vanilla that always gave her an untamed, raw sexiness he knew she wasn't aware of. There'd been moments during the evening when he'd barely been able to restrain himself from cutting short the meal so that he could get her back to the palace and make love to her. He just had to think about the feel of her breasts in his hands and his pulses went into freefall.

He didn't want to talk about her returning to London, even though it had been on his mind. Of course, everything she'd said had made perfect sense, and he should have been grateful that she was adopting such a pragmatic approach to a future that wasn't going to conveniently disappear just because he wasn't quite ready for it to overtake him. Not just yet. Not when he still burned for her.

Malik was accustomed to taking the lead when it came to ending relationships. This time, he'd found himself acquiescing to someone else's common sense and he was finding that he had to grit his teeth through it. Was it selfish of him to want more of her? He had to remind himself that his life was now going down a different road, the only road he was prepared to go down.

He *would* marry a suitable woman. The time had come, and he *would* step up to the plate and do his duty without flinching.

Lucy was a ship passing in the night and, as they'd both admitted, what she wanted was out of reach with him, so all he could do was wish her well in her search for Mr Right.

It was annoying that a part of him was a little piqued at her easy acceptance of the situation. He was ashamed to think that that might just be his ego talking. The shoe was on the other foot and he didn't like it.

'I don't think my father would recognise a golf club if I put one in front of him,' Malik mused, feasting on her prettiness and feeling the stir of his body responding. He noted the way her eyes darkened as they tangled with his. When he lowered his gaze to her thighs, she blushed but didn't look away. 'Once upon a distant time, he used to be quite passable at polo.'

'Really? Isn't that said to be the sport of kings?'

'Not kings in their sixties who are recuperating from heart problems.'

'You can be pretty funny when you put your mind to it.'

'I do my best.'

'How will he spend all the free time he'll be finding himself with?'

'Both my parents do a considerable amount of charity work with various other countries and kingdoms in the area. They're very much into promoting clean drinking water, irrigation and schooling for outposts that are located far from the cities.'

'That's amazing.'

'Yes. Yes, it is.'

'Will you and your wife…er…continue with that tradition?'

'Lucy, I haven't even met this so-called woman who will be entering my life. How on earth could I have had discussions with her about what she would or wouldn't like to do?'

'Just asking.'

'This isn't how I envisaged the evening ending up.'

'That's because when you're with me all you think about is sex.'

'That's not true!' Malik said in a low, outraged voice. 'You and I have a hell of a lot more between us than *just sex*.'

'Do we?'

'What's going on with you, Lucy? Why are you suddenly determined to pick an argument with me after the fantastic evening we've just had?'

'It's not unreasonable to ask a few questions. I'm not going to just live in a vacuum until I wake up one morning to find that my suitcase has been pulled out of the wardrobe and my airline ticket is on the dressing table. A week and a half isn't very long. I can start putting things in place, if that's a definite timeline.'

Malik flung his hands in the air in an exasperated gesture and glared at her. 'How is it possible to be one hundred perfect definite in this? How much time will your sister need to get to the corner shop for the pint of milk?' He looked at her with brooding intensity. 'Maybe I won't find anyone. Maybe this thing we have between us…isn't…'

'Isn't what?'

'You look at me and I burn for you,' Malik muttered, every word sounding as though it was being dragged out of him. 'When we first… I didn't expect the ferocity of this. Maybe I can delay the whole marriage thing for a while…'

'I don't think so, Malik.'

'What do you mean by that?'

'This isn't going to play out on your terms and your terms only.'

'Did I ever say that it would?'

'You know, growing up in a big family, you had to make yourself heard; you had to be able to stand up for yourself and not let other people make decisions for you. So, now?' Lucy sighed. 'I can't just hang around until you get me out of your system.'

Malik flushed darkly.

'I don't like the way that makes me sound.'

'But,' she said gently, 'You *are* a guy who's accustomed to getting his own way, aren't you? With women… in business…in life in general. You mentioned a ball; is there a date set for it?'

'It's next Saturday.'

'Hence the week and a half guideline,' Lucy said. 'Is that what tonight was all about?'

'What do you mean?' There was genuine bewilderment in his voice.

'Tonight…it really *was* wonderful, Malik, and something I'll remember for ever…but was it your last hurrah?'

'No idea what you're talking about.'

'Was this the last big gesture before we wrap things up?'

'That's not why I did tonight. I… I wanted to show you my country…what it's like in the desert at night… and I wanted to do it in style.'

Malik stilled as he looked back at the evening they had spent together. He had arranged the whole thing himself, including arranging which chefs should prepare the food. The whole thing had smacked of romance, and for a few seconds he'd been taken aback by the sheer pleasure that afforded him.

Him, the guy who didn't do *romance*.

And now he was here, wanting more.

Habits conditioned over a lifetime kicked in with force, because he could remember the bitterness of realising the truth about life—that allowing emotions free rein was a recipe for disaster. Especially for a man in his position, where duty to his country and the responsibilities of his blood line were vital. He was a guy who, at all times, needed to put his head above emotion. But what he felt here, sitting in the back seat of his car, caught up in this conversation with a woman he couldn't get enough of… It made him *vulnerable* and that was not going to do. Just contemplating that sign of weakness was enough to make his blood run cold.

'But of course you're right,' he said coolly, back in a place of control. 'You need a deadline. My parents are expecting you at the ball. It will be a grand affair and a good opportunity for you to meet a lot of people who have considerable financial concerns in London. A great chance to network. I will do my bit, and you can put it in the bracket of giving you a good reference. Day after, I'll make sure that you're booked first class to return to London.'

They stared at each other in silence for a few seconds that seemed to go on for ever.

'Sounds good,' Lucy murmured, the first to look away. 'That will give my sister plenty of time to get the pint of milk in.'

CHAPTER NINE

IT WAS A curious mix of feelings: utter sadness, fierce determination to keep smiling, a powerful sense of inevitability and the promise of despair waiting just over the horizon. This was the swirl of emotions Lucy felt as she stared down at the dress on her bed, waiting to be worn to the ball that awaited her in less than an hour and a half.

The remaining time they'd had together had shot by. It was as though, having put a timeline to everything, the ticking hands of the clock had sped up, determined to make sure that nothing came in the way of the parting of their ways.

Work had been side-lined by both of them. Of course, they'd done what was necessary but, without any conscious agreement, life had taken on the tenor of a holiday.

Malik had showed her Sarastan. She'd been awed by the dunes but she'd discovered that there was much more to his beautiful country than the rolling, ever-changing hills of sand beyond the walls of his magnificent palace. The city was modern and vibrant. The hotels were amazing, and they'd gone for dinner and drinks at several of them, once staying overnight because the hot temptation of bed had proved too much at a little past eleven in the evening.

Lucy had told him that she'd never seen so much marble, hanging crystal and over-sized indoor plants before in her life when they'd dined at one of the five-star hotels in the heart of the bustling city.

He's taken her to the old town, where markets and bartering were very different from the high-end malls stuffed with designer goods. And they'd gone to the coast, which was empty, quiet and quite spectacular. The sea was warm, and Lucy had swum until she was exhausted; then they'd lain down, staring up at the turquoise sky, lost in their own private thoughts.

She'd been thinking that job hunting in London was going to be a painful ordeal after this. She'd glimpsed paradise, had tasted paradise, and nothing would ever compete.

She hadn't breathed a word about Malik to any of her sisters, but she *had* told Helen, even though she'd been loath to unburden herself when her friend had been all angst about giving birth in a fortnight. In due course, she would confess everything to her family, but only after she was on the road to recovery.

The sight of the dress on the bed brought her back to reality with a thump because she had under an hour to get ready. She would be chauffeured to his parents' palace.

Malik was already there, having gone ahead to start the process of mingling. She had forced herself not to pepper him with questions about what that entailed because she wasn't interested in hearing the answer. However, her imagination had not held back in painting very colourful scenarios that involved him being introduced to a mile-long queue of eligible beauties, all breathlessly excited at being chosen to be a princess by the knight in shining armour.

On the spur of the moment, she picked up the dainty sandals she had bought and flung one against the wall, which it hit with absolutely no force before dropping to the ground, and thankfully not falling apart, because there were no alternative options in her wardrobe.

She showered in record time, applied her make-up and did her hair—the little that could be done with it—before stepping into the gown she had bought on one of their trips to the city centre. It was a long, layered affair in shades of blues and greens. The neckline was modest, the dainty straps were very demure and it just *fell*, only clinging slightly under the bust.

Yet, as Lucy stood back to inspect herself in the full-length mirror, she felt as though it was all just a little bit *too much*. Her boobs looked enormous, for starters. She'd been seduced by the Grecian style of the long dress but now had to conclude that Grecian women clearly didn't have big bosoms.

Her hair… Well, it was too late to do anything with it, although on impulse she fished out a couple of pearly clips and strung some of it back so that only escaping tendrils fell across her face.

The driver was there and waiting by the time she made it down and half an hour later, as the black Bentley made its way up the familiar courtyard that formed an enormous circle outside the palace, her heart was beating like a sledgehammer. There were lots of cars and none of them were old bangers. There were also lots of people, in an array of clothing, from traditional white robes to designer suits—dashing men and women dressed to kill, draped in jewellery and sheathed in the finest silks.

The palace was lit up like a Christmas tree and there were uniformed staff everywhere. All that seemed to be missing was a red carpet.

Malik had given her the option of just not coming.

'It's not a necessity,' he had told her gruffly, a few days ago as they'd lain in bed, wrapped round one another, bodies so entwined that they couldn't have slipped a piece of paper between them.

'Wouldn't your parents be a little surprised?'

'I'm sure they could survive the disappointment.'

'You think I'm going to be upset, don't you? Because there'll be all those hopeful beauties there, waiting for you to chat them up.'

'Won't you?'

'Not a bit of it,' Lucy had returned stoutly. 'I'll have my own queue of hopefuls desperate to be my Prince Charming when I get back to London.'

He hadn't said anything.

Truth was, she *knew* that he felt she'd find it hard to deal with the situation, whatever she said to the contrary. The mere fact that she'd come to that conclusion made Lucy all the more determined to show up, even if it damn well killed her.

There was also the bracing thought that seeing Malik

in action, seeing him embrace this final chapter in their relationship, the chapter in which he moved on, was *necessary*. It would be a healthy dose of reality. She would see him chatting to the woman he would eventually marry, and any rose-tinted spectacles she might be wearing would very quickly be ripped off her.

'Right,' she muttered under her breath as the Bentley slowly circled the courtyard, coming to a gradual stop outside the imposing front door, which had been flung open. 'Show time.'

On either side was uniformed staff, several of them. Lucy edged her way out, took a deep breath and decided that the very first thing she would do was help herself to a little bit of Dutch courage…

Inside the ballroom Malik tugged at the black bow-tie and helped himself to his second glass of champagne. He had expected nothing less than perfection, and perfection was what had awaited him when he'd arrived at his parents' sumptuous palace a couple of hours earlier.

Yes, last-minute things were still being done, but the wing in which the party was being held had been kitted out in regal style. Purple and white flowers wound like ivy around the multiple white pillars in the room; stunted palm trees in golden pots had been lugged in for special effect and some poor souls had spent hours buffing the many chandeliers. Waiters circulated with a giddy array of canapés and there was no end to the champagne.

At a little past seven, the guests arrived thick and fast. Many of them were esteemed families, all known to Malik, as were their kids, whose ages more or less aligned with his, from early twenties to mid-thirties. He had played rugby with a few of the guys and catching up was good.

There would be no formal introductions, his mother had assured him. In a rare moment of physical affection, she had adjusted his bow-tie, stepped back and told him that he should just enjoy the evening. Malik had wryly thought that it was hardly what he would have described as a relaxing social event, but he had smiled, nodded and told her that he would do just that.

Was he relaxing? He sipped his champagne. From where he was standing, back to one of the walls, he had a wide-angled view. The ballroom led off to various other rooms, all buzzing. There were ample, plush seating areas. There were two billiard tables in another room, with a groaning bar behind which several uniformed waiters were ready and eager to pour drinks, and there were ornately dressed tables laden with the finest food money could buy, served by an army of waiters.

He'd been introduced to several women. To a fault, they had demurely pretended that theirs was a polite, perfunctory introduction rather than a targeted meet-and-greet that could lead to matrimony with the kingdom's most eligible bachelor. They were all dressed traditionally and ornately in silks of quiet, restrained colours, abundant amounts of jewellery, lavish but cleverly applied make-up and were groomed beautifully to within an inch of their lives.

They were beautiful, subservient women who would all make a fantastic wife for a man like him: powerful, wealthy, leading a high-octane, high-stress life laden with responsibilities. A man who would require a sub-servient wife, a wife whose soothing personality would ease away the tensions of the day.

Additionally, of course, a wife who would know the ropes because it would be what she had grown up with. Someone who would realise that his workload would always come first, be they in London or Sarastan, because much of it involved the livelihoods of many other people, employees in the hundreds who worked in the factories and businesses owned and run by the Al-Rashid family. She would not expect declarations of love or the heady excitement of romantic gestures.

Whoever he chose would be like his parents: practicality before impulse, head before heart. In short, the ideal woman would know that unreasonable demands would not be in the picture.

Malik wondered where the hell Lucy was. He didn't realise that his eyes were trained on the door until he saw her and then he straightened and sucked in his breath. For a few wild seconds, his thoughts were all over the place, making a mockery of the very reason he was at this event: to find a suitable wife with charac-teristics and traits he had already painstakingly bullet-pointed in his head only moments before.

She looked extravagantly pretty. Next to the highly polished perfection of the women he had met, she looked so natural that it took his breath away.

Her hair was a tumble of blonde curls, some of it tied back but still falling around her heart-shaped face. Her face was smooth, with just a bit of colour on her cheeks and her perfect, full mouth. The colour on her cheeks might have been accentuated by her clear discomfort as she stood still, looking around her hesitantly and clutching a small blue-and-gold bag with a chain strap.

Malik couldn't quite get himself to move as he continued to look at her. The dress was magnificent. She'd taken herself off shopping, laughing when he'd offered to go with her, telling him that she was actually clever enough to make her way through some shops and whether or not he liked what she tried on wouldn't determine what she bought. The dress was a gentle swirl of blues and greens and outlined the generous rounded breasts that he had only recently lost himself in. Her curves were lovingly outlined by the sheer fabric.

She looked like a goddess and, as fast as his libido started rising at speed, he told himself that this was not appropriate. Their time was at an end. This was always going to be nothing more than a fling. Her appearance here was the final piece of a jigsaw that should never have been started. But he would never bring himself to regret it.

He pushed himself from the wall and began weaving his way towards her, only stopping halfway when he felt a gentle hand on his arm and looked down to see one of the women he had previously chatted to smiling up at him.

What was her name… Irena?

'There's going to be dancing, Malik.'

'Huh?' Malik tugged the bow-tie looser and then frowned when she straightened it back into position.

'Dancing, in the conservatory. The band's going to be setting up in an hour.'

'Terrific.'

He smiled to be polite, but he was impatient to rescue Lucy from her awkward dithering at the edge of the crowd.

She usually appeared so confident, even though he had learned from knowing her that the confidence was usually only skin-deep. Right now, it was clear that she couldn't even muster up the skin-deep veneer of confidence.

It was his duty to rescue her. They might have said goodbye to their brief liaison but he was still her employer, still responsible for her and, it might be said, still caring and thoughtful enough to want to make her feel less ill at ease amongst this glamorous crowd of people.

Boosted by that positive thought, yet not wishing to offend anyone—least of all this very attractive girl who was gazing up at him with expectation—Malik murmured something and nothing at her coy request that he save the first dance for her.

'Isn't it the last dance that's supposed to be saved, according to the song?'

She gave him look, polite, still smiling but puzzled, and he agreed to do just that before hurriedly moving away before Lucy could do something stupid like take flight and disappear.

From across the room—trying hard not to look as though she was looking around her, because she was lost and wanted to turn tail and flee—Lucy's gaze finally alighted on Malik.

She stilled and could feel the slow burn of colour creeping into her cheeks. This was exactly what she wanted and needed, wasn't it? Just what she'd told herself was necessary—ripping those damn rose-tinted specs from her eyes. Seeing him in action at this event where his bride would be chosen.

Yet, her heart constricted and she wanted the ground to open up and swallow her. Love was a steady, painful thump inside her and she blinked, only to see that he had broken up talking to someone so that he could dutifully wend his way towards her.

Was the woman one of the many hopefuls? Even a quick glance around her was enough to tell her that the place was teeming with hopefuls, and the hopefuls were all so staggeringly beautiful that he would have to have been a fool not to find someone here that fitted the bill.

What fitting the bill might entail, exactly, she had no idea because it was a topic that had been very firmly on the list of things that were forbidden to talk about.

The woman in question was tall and slender and looked to be in her early twenties, with raven-dark hair artfully swept up into something very clever that was threaded with lovely glittering jewels. Her dress was a simple black-and-gold affair. And her skin was flawless.

Lucy wished she had had the foresight to apply some fake tan for the occasion, then told herself not to be utterly ridiculous.

'Lucy.'

Lucy looked up at a Malik, who took her breath away.

He was in dark trousers with a white shirt and a bow-tie. Where the jacket of the tuxedo was, she had no idea— probably discarded somewhere.

The bow-tie would have meta similar fate, she was sure, had it not been for the solicitations of the dark-haired beauty he'd been chatting to who had helpfully put it back in place.

She watched with a jaundiced eye as he began to yank it off.

'Damn thing's strangling me.'

'Oh, dear. Still, it's a good ploy.'

'What do you mean?'

'I mean it's certainly a clever way to get the ladies here jumping over each other to straighten it out.'

A waiter swung by with a tray filled with glasses of champagne and Lucy quickly nabbed a flute and took a few sips, while glancing around her—anywhere but at Malik.

Her heart was beating so fast she could feel it try-ing to fly right out of her chest. She could breathe him in and his unique musky, woody, intensely masculine aroma made her nostrils flare.

'This is all very magnificent, Malik. Your parents must have slaved day and night to put this all together.'

'Or employed people who did. Are you okay?'

'Of course I am! Why shouldn't I be?' Her champagne glass seemed to be empty.

'You drank that pretty quickly. You're nervous. I don't blame you. Look, let me introduce you to a few people. You'll find that they largely all speak fluent English.'

He half-turned but she remained put and he raised his eyebrows in a question.

'You don't have to tear yourself away from your own party to show me around, Malik. I'm fine making my way through the crowds.'

'Don't be silly. You don't know a soul here.'

'I know your mother.'

'I thought that this might be a bad idea.'

'What are you talking about?'

'It's awkward for you, Lucy. I get that.' He raked his fingers through his hair and whipped off the bow-tie completely, shoving it in his pocket.

'Well,' Lucy was appalled to hear herself say, 'There goes *that* golden opportunity for an attractive woman to fiddle around with you...'

'Lucy!'

'I'm sorry. That was uncalled for. She's very beautiful and she looks incredibly sweet.'

'Are you jealous?'

'No,' she lied. 'Maybe just a little. But don't worry. It doesn't mean that I'm not going to have a good time while I'm here, and you won't have to be anxious that I've glued myself to a wall somewhere because I'm too timid to do the rounds.'

Malik looked at her in silence for so long that she began to fidget.

'Well...' She backed away and gave him an airy wave of her fingers. 'I shall go and pay my respects to your parents and then disappear into the crowd.'

'I doubt you'll be able to pull off a disappearing act in that outfit,' Malik ground out.

* * *

For the first time since he'd come here, he felt *alive*.

He could barely remember what the woman who'd playfully adjusted his bow-tie had looked like because he only had eyes for the woman standing in front of him. And that was a weakness he did not want to indulge.

They'd done what they'd done, but they'd both set their parameters, and he wasn't going to let a little physical weakness lead him astray.

'Thanks a lot, Malik!'

Lucy began to spin away but he reached out and circled his hand around her wrist, stilling her.

'You don't understand what I mean by that,' he said in a roughened undertone.

'I know exactly what you mean! You mean that, alongside all these sophisticated beauties with pedigrees as long as your arm, I look like a fool!'

'The opposite, for God's sake!'

'What do you mean?'

'You know exactly what I mean, Lucy.'

'No. I don't!'

'I mean you stand there and everyone else is in the shade! No one can miss you because you look sexy as hell!'

He whipped his hand away and stood back but he couldn't tear his eyes away from her.

He'd meant every word, but none of those words should have been spoken because none of them was appropriate, given the circumstances.

'My mother is in the sitting area,' he said unevenly.

'Let me…let me take you there—introduce you to some of her friends…'

'I'm fine,' Lucy shot back, tilting her chin and taking two steps away from him. 'You go and do what you have to do!'

Lucy knew how to mingle. Coming from a big family, where every event seemed to involve half the neighbourhood and so many extended family members that elbow room had to be fought for, mingling came naturally to her. Plus, she wanted to make sure that Malik didn't see her skulking somewhere, nursing her hurt and her wounded heart.

No, not her *wounded* heart. Her utterly destroyed and broken heart. She comforted herself with what he'd said about her looking sexy, but then told herself that that meant nothing.

Out of the corner of her eye, she always seemed to have him in her line of vision, noticing the way people flocked to him, male and female.

This was his *home*, she thought miserably. This was where he *belonged*. London had just borrowed him for a moment in time and soon the beautiful woman who had done his bow tie, who seemed to be next to him whenever Lucy looked in his direction, would anchor him back in his heartland.

Her smile was glassy as she mingled with everyone. The food was exquisite, and she filled her plate and sat with a lovely group of people at one of the many circular tables, but she barely tasted a thing. She knew that she was operating on automatic. She heard herself laughing and asking interested questions. Champagne flowed in her direction until she was woozy…and more miserable.

And ever more aware of the young, smiling brunette with the fabulous slender body who had attached herself to Malik. Who knew what he thought about *that* situation? Was the brunette to be *the one*…while Lucy returned to his palace with her airline ticket waiting for her, all booked for two days' time?

At the stroke of midnight, with reckless abandon, Lucy weaved her way to thank his parents for having her and, that duty under her belt, she headed towards Malik.

Of course, she should thank him for asking her along. He'd offered to be the solicitous host and it wasn't his fault that she'd turned her back on that act of charity.

Thanks, but no thanks.

But thank him politely she would! She knew exactly when he spotted her because at that very moment the group around him, including the brunette, seemed to perform a convenient vanishing act.

One simple 'thanks, and hope to see you before I leave the country' and she'd be gone—out of his life for ever, with just one backward glance at a life left behind when she went to clear her stuff from the offices in London.

'Lucy.'

His deep, dark, familiar, outrageously sexy voice brought the glaze of tears to her eyes.

'You don't have to…' she heard herself say and, when he looked at her enquiringly, she added for good measure, 'Marry someone you don't want to marry. You don't have to do that.'

And there it was—out in the open. All the love and longing she felt for him.

She squeezed her eyes tightly shut and, honest to the last, she breathed with heartfelt sincerity. 'I love you, Malik.'

She looked at him, appalled by what she could hear herself saying, but driven to speak her mind before she disappeared out of his life for ever. To hell with stupid consequences. What more could happen? It wasn't as though she'd have to face him across a desk any longer.

'Don't marry her. Marry me.'

She watched as he turned his head away. He clenched his jaw, and when he looked at her his dark eyes were blank of expression.

'Lucy…'

'No. Don't say anything.'

'I'm sorry.'

CHAPTER TEN

MALIK COULDN'T MOVE a muscle as he watched her swiftly disappear, eaten up by all the people still there, including Irena, who had dutifully hunted him out for the first dance she had insisted he save for her. When he'd glanced across the space that had been set up for the young people to dance, Lucy was nowhere to be seen.

He'd known what she was going to say before she'd uttered those three killer words. He'd seen it in her eyes and had been pole-axed. Should he have seen that coming? They'd made a pact but pacts were often broken. He should know all about that because it had happened before—women given boundaries, only for him to find that the boundaries had become too onerous for them somewhere along the way.

But for Lucy to tell him that she loved him...

He had pulled away at speed.

No! That had *never* been on the cards. He wasn't after that. He was after the sanity and practicality of a marriage based on cool reason, with a woman who would understand the life they were signing up to.

A woman like Irena.

He forced himself to remain at his own ball for another couple of hours, making sure to disentangle himself from making any arrangements to do anything with any woman. Time enough for those sorts of life-changing decisions! Meanwhile, he would have to let his blood cool in the wake of Lucy's confession.

He knew when she was leaving because he'd handled booking the ticket himself: first-class direct flight in two days, mid-morning.

In the meantime, he would do them both a favour and lay low, which was easy, given he had a suite of rooms in the city centre. By the time he returned to London, she would be gone. He knew when she intended to go to the office to clear her things. He would give her the chance and the privacy to do that without having to look him in the face.

She was proud and he imagined she would be embarrassed by what she'd confessed. He could tell her that it would have been the champagne talking, but why not spare them both the awkwardness of circling around one another, both sharing the same place until she left where memories of what they'd had would be everywhere?

He found himself drinking way too much for his liking for what remained of the evening, and had a thick head when he awoke the following morning in his apartment in the city. It was a different bed, different décor with no warm, yielding, sexy body to wrap his arms around, to breathe in, to caress.

He was still in bed at close to ten when his phone beeped, and when he looked it was to see a text from Lucy.

Changed my flight. Leaving in a couple of hours. I'll clear my stuff out of the office tomorrow evening. It's Sunday and no one will be around. Take care and good luck with the rest of your life.

His eyes felt damp when he pressed his thumbs over them.

Of course they weren't tears—it was fatigue. And too much champagne, followed by whisky—an unfortunate combination. Why would he cry when this was exactly what he had planned from the outset?

Yet the pain was unbearable. All those years of telling himself that he was invincible when it came to his emotion washed away in a tide of suffocating sorrow.

What the hell had he done?

He knew exactly what he'd done. He'd bought into his own misconception that he was immune to love; that what he felt for Lucy was something he could control; that his head was always going to have the final say, because that was what he had stupidly decided would always be the best outcome for him.

Now, in the loneliness of his luxurious apartment, all he could feel was the misery of his own wrong turns and bad decisions. He'd been blind when he'd assumed that all he felt for her was lust. He'd conveniently forgotten the way she'd made him smile, the way she'd made him feel warm and satisfied inside. Love had spouted tentacles long before they'd slept together, but he just hadn't seen it, and now...

He pressed his thumbs to his eyes again and felt the

dampness of heartache tearing through him, leaking from his eyes.

Time to fix this. Or was everything lost for ever?

Once back in London, Lucy felt as though Sarastan and everything that had happened there had been a dream. A dream dreamt a thousand years ago when she'd been a different person from the one who now stood here, in her box in North London, unpacking her suitcase and gazing around her at surroundings that couldn't have been further removed from the one she had left behind.

She was really tired. She'd managed to change the flight without any trouble at all. Actually, they knew who had booked it, and she felt if she'd shown up at one in the morning the staff there would have found a private jet, such was the power of the Al-Rashid name.

Malik.

God. She couldn't believe what she'd told him. Was there *anything* to be said for acting on impulse?

And yet, telling him how she felt about him had been cleansing. She hadn't meant to; she had always planned to leave with her head held high and her love firmly under wraps.

But then…there, at the ball and in the moment…it had all been too much.

Love had burst the barriers. Seeing him in the life he was going to be leading, away from her for ever, hadn't been the salutary lesson she'd been hoping for. It hadn't set her on the straight and narrow. It had just been a cruel reminder of what she was about to lose—the only man she could ever see herself loving.

She'd maintained her stiff upper lip all the way back to the palace. The driver who had brought her to the ball had been waiting to return her to Malik's palace and the last thing she'd needed was to sob her way noisily all the way back.

But, as soon as she'd got back to her suite of rooms, the tears had come, a river of them, great, heaving sobs followed by horrible nausea, thanks to too much champagne.

Still, she'd woken the following morning and, despite the thick head, she had packed fast, taken a couple of tablets and phoned to change her flight. The thought of bumping into Malik had panicked her—no need, as it had turned out.

She'd been prepared to tiptoe her way down, but the place had been quiet and, out of curiosity, she'd tiptoed to his rooms to find that he wasn't there. He hadn't come back at all, and that had cut her to the quick, because where had he spent the night?

At his parents'? Or with someone else? With the brunette? Surely not? That would surely have been frowned upon, but then was she really up and running about how modern or not the women in Sarastan were? Who knew what they got up to, tradition or no tradition? They could hit the local pole dancing clubs when the sun set, for all she knew.

Which thought made her smile for a minute or two.

She would give all those summery, optimistic dresses to charity so that there were no visible reminders of her time out there, and then she would head to the office to clear her stuff. Sunday would be a brilliant day to do that because there would be no curious eyes, no questions. She'd be able to disappear without any fuss.

In the morning, she would do a food shop and then head in to the office—it would be safer in the evening. Hedge-fund managers in charge of billions often had an annoying habits of working at the weekend but no one worked on a Sunday evening. That was beyond the pale.

And yet…

It had been oh, so easy to be calm and collected from the safety of her box in Swiss Cottage. Broken hearts were so much easier to nurse when there were no reminders around.

Just heading in on the Tube was a reminder of the familiar route she would be leaving behind. Her feet slowed as they approached the impressive, towering building that housed Malik's elite task force. The sun had set and it was very quiet. Groups and couples were drifting along, heading for who knew what restaurant, bar or evening dinner party somewhere?

It was chilly. Even through her jeans and the old jumper she had flung on she could still feel the cold nipping at her.

Deep breath.

She was already taking out the two bin bags she had brought with her as she pushed through the revolving door into the foyer where Sam, the guy at front desk at the weekend, smiled and tried to engage her in conversation.

'Just clearing a few things,' she said chirpily, but her smile was glazed and her eyes were a little unfocused.

He looked puzzled.

Probably thinks I'm nuts, Lucy thought as the lift pinged on its way up. Too bad; in half an hour, she'd be on her way out and that would be the end of that.

She stared down at the ground of the silent, deserted office as she made her way to Malik's office suite, which was past the central area with its minimalist furnishings and its state-of-the-art computers, all now switched off.

She banged lights on as she went. She took a deep breath as she stood outside Malik's office and then opened the door and stepped in to a darkened room— her outer office, where over the years she had accumulated, frankly, the sort of bric-a-brac that her sisters would fondly have laughed at. There were framed photos, plants, an array of pens in cases, because who could resist a decent, colourful pencil case? There were some little ceramic *objets d'art* which were great for fiddling around with when she was bored and taking a quick break.

She banged on the light and there was her desk, as clear as she had left it weeks ago…bar the massive wrapped box on top.

It was in silver wrapping with a big red bow.

She stared, frozen to the spot.

What the heck was this and what the heck was going on?

Inside his office, where he had been sitting for the past two and a half hours, Malik vaulted upright the minute Lucy switched on the outside light.

He'd never felt more nervous.

Watch and wait…? See what happened when she opened that box…? No, that felt a little too voyeuristic, although it was cravenly tempting.

He pushed open the door, cleared his throat and then they were looking at one another. Her face was a picture of open-mouthed shock. Her big, blue eyes were wide with absolute astonishment.

'Lucy…'

'What are you doing here?'

'I… Why don't you sit down? Before you fall down.' He moved forward quickly, dragged her leather chair out from behind her desk and rolled it over to where she hadn't moved a muscle since she'd entered the room.

'What are you doing here?' she again demanded shrilly, ignoring the chair. 'Why have you come here? You *knew* I'd be here collecting my stuff, Malik! Why have you picked now to show up?'

'Because…' He faltered to a stop but then nodded to the box on her desk. 'Lucy, would you open the box? It's…something I bought for you…'

'Tripped up at the last minute by a guilty conscience, Malik?' she asked with dripping sarcasm.

Galvanised into action, she strode over to her desk, ignoring both him and the chair, and yanked open the drawers to begin the process of stuffing her belongings into one of the bin bags.

'No need to feel guilty,' she muttered in a driven undertone. 'No need to feel sorry for me. I'm quite capable of moving on from you, whatever you might think.'

'What you said…'

'What about it?' She stopped to glare at him but even

in mid-glare she noted that he looked haggard. 'And how the heck did you manage to get here so fast?' she demanded accusingly. 'Last time I saw you, you were about to disappear back into your "find a bride" party.'

Her eyes blurred with tears.

'I didn't disappear back into it for long,' Malik admitted roughly. 'You left me…you walked away… I went to my place in the city centre. You asked how I got here? Private jet. I didn't have the patience to go through the usual channels. I had to get here…had to see you…'

'And now you have. So, you can disappear back to Sarastan in your private jet and pick up where you left off there!'

She was being horrible but how could she help it? How could she be expected to hang on to her self-control when he was standing in the room like her very worst nightmare come to life.

'Did you mean it? What you said…about loving me…'

Lucy stared, livid that he had asked that, livid that he was here and yet unable to deny the truth of what she had told him.

'What does it matter?'

'A lot. The box…it's not a guilt gift, Lucy. Please… would you open it?'

So, she did. She reckoned that she might as well, because the faster she could leave, the better. She couldn't do this. Couldn't be in the same room as Malik.

It was an enormous box and she wondered whether he'd thoughtlessly decided to get her a farewell gift of a new laptop for whatever new job she managed to find.

She began tearing off the paper—thick, expensive paper, she couldn't help but notice *en passant*. The bow got chucked on the ground. She could feel his dark eyes on her and, when she quickly glanced up at him, she shivered because she couldn't read what he was thinking, not at all.

And she'd always been half-decent at doing that.

The paper kept coming off, layer upon layer upon layer, and then, just when she was about to give up in tearful, angry frustration and misery, there it was—a little black velvet box which she stared down at without touching.

'What's this?' she asked suspiciously.

'Open it.'

'Tell me.' But she was already flipping open the little box, and there it was—a ring...with a diamond on it. The purest, most beautiful diamond she had ever seen in her life. Not that she'd seen very many, actually.

'What's this?' she repeated, but her voice was hesitant, although she couldn't staunch the rush of excitement that threaded its way through her.

She trembled as he took a few steps towards her until he was right next to her, so close to her that she could reach out and touch him.

'Will you marry me, Lucy?'

'Sorry?' She blinked and wondered whether she'd misheard or else maybe hallucinated something she *wanted* to hear as opposed to what she *actually* heard.

'I want you to be my wife. Will you marry me?'

'Will I *marry* you? How can you ask that when

you're already involved in the process of marrying someone else?'

'Let's sit. This conversation…isn't one to be had standing up, staring at one another with a desk at the side. Makes me think I should be dictating something for you to transcribe.' He smiled tentatively, crookedly, but he didn't move, waiting to see what she would do.

Since her legs were beginning to feel like jelly, Lucy shuffled to the sofa by the wall and fell into it. Her heart was pounding and her thoughts were all over the place. She'd left the little box with the twinkling diamond right where it was on the desk and now she longed to cast another eye over it to make sure she wasn't dreaming.

He sat next to her, not too close but not too far. Close enough to touch, but only if he reached out—no place for any accidental brushing of hands.

They stared at one another.

'You're shocked.'

'Are you surprised?'

'No.'

'The last time I saw you, you were telling me in no uncertain terms just how you felt about me.' Her voice was laced with bitterness and, however much the diamond ring was calling, she wasn't going to pay heed to the temptation to listen to that siren call. *No, sir.*

'Lucy,' he said heavily, and this time he did lean forward. 'I always knew the path I was going to follow. Especially after my youthful…what shall I call it?…*misjudgement*, well, I accepted that love and romance, and all the complications that came with that, were never going to feature in my life.' He sighed. 'I knew what my parents had and I knew that it was a formula that worked—an arranged marriage with no room for misunderstandings. When we…started what we started…'

Lucy stiffened but didn't pull away when he hesitantly reached across to link his fingers through hers.

'Go on,' she said tersely. 'I'm listening. *Just about.*'

Malik smiled. 'Everything about you is so wonderfully unique, Lucy. The fact that I've always thought that should have been a clue as to how I really felt about you.'

'And which is how, exactly?'

Lucy wanted to sound sharp, but instead sounded hopeful, so she glowered to make up for the weakness, which made him smile just a little bit more.

'Dependent,' he said simply.

'Dependent…?'

'I'm in love with you, my darling, and if I didn't have the courage or the wit to see that before then I am happy to spend the rest of my life apologising for the oversight.' He looked at her with utter seriousness.

'But what about all those plans you made? The ball? What about that brunette you spent the entire evening with? I half-expected an announcement to be made by the end of the evening!'

'That was never going to happen,' Malik said wryly. 'It wasn't a fairy tale story to be wrapped up in a few chapters with a wedding at the end. The only woman I had eyes for at that ball was *you*. The only woman's voice I wanted to hear was yours. The only woman I wanted to spend the rest of my life with… I realised… was *you*. So, did you mean what you said about loving me? I've been a fool, but will you have me now? Will you forgive me my blindness?'

Lucy smiled.

She clasped his hands with hers and leant towards him to brush his cheek with her fingers. That dear, dear face that she knew so well. How could she ever have imagined that what they'd shared could be left behind? He might have been blind to what he'd felt, but she'd been blind as well in assuming that what *she* felt could be contained. Somewhere along the line, attraction had cemented into something solid and wonderful, and she'd chosen to overlook that because she hadn't wanted to admit to it.

So would she marry him—this big, complex, strong, vulnerable guy she'd fallen head over heels in love with?

'Forgive your blindness? I think I can do that… I've been a fool as well for ever thinking that I could get you out of my system. Once you entered it, you were always going to be there for ever. And as for marrying you…?' She dimpled in the way he had fallen for from day one. 'I think there might just be a space in my diary…'

EPILOGUE

'MY MOTHER,' MALIK SAID, turning on his side to look at his adored wife, who was busy reading an interior design magazine, 'Wants to know whether a palace is too extravagant a gift for our son.'

Lucy dumped the magazine on the table at the side of the enormous four-poster bed, which had been their top priority for the house they had bought four months previously 'Our son…has yet to be born…'

She grinned and watched with a burst of love as Malik curved his hand over the swell of her belly.

She was eight months' pregnant and was quietly amused that her husband seemed a lot more nervous about the impending birth of their baby boy than she. He'd made her pack her hospital bag over six weeks ago, even though she had rolled her eyes and told him that he was being over-dramatic.

The past few months had shot past. They had married and the wedding had been wonderful and intimate, with just close friends and family invited. Lucy had fretted that, after the magnificence of what an arranged wedding would have looked like, his parents would be bitterly disappointed. In her usual forthright way, she had aired her concerns with his mother, with whom she had developed a wonderfully close bond.

But not a bit of it. Nadia had confided that she and Ali would have adored something a lot less spectacular, but in the end they had followed tradition and done what had been expected.

Bit by bit, Malik was opening his eyes to what Lucy had gathered pretty much as soon as she had got to know his parents. They might have had an arranged marriage but within that arrangement was a bedrock of love, something Malik had never really seen.

She covered his hand with hers and then shuffled over to kiss him lightly on the mouth as he continued to caress her naked belly.

'I think a toy palace would work very well in due course.' She gazed at Malik lovingly. 'Even though I know your mum and dad are thinking about the real deal.'

'It'll be very hard not to spoil him.' Malik paused and smiled. 'Just as it's bloody impossible not to spoil *you*, when you let me.'

'You already spoil me enough.'

'You refuse diamonds and pearls.'

'I have everything I could ever need.' She stroked his cheek and felt their baby move in her tummy, preparing to join them, to make them a family of three. 'I have you…'

* * * * *

If you just couldn't put down Royally Promoted,
then you're sure to love the first instalment in the
Secrets of Billionaires' Secretaries duet,
A Wedding Negotiation with Her Boss*!*

And why not dive into these other stories
by Cathy Williams?

A Week with the Forbidden Greek
The Housekeeper's Invitation to Italy
The Italian's Innocent Cinderella
Unveiled as the Italian's Bride
Bound by Her Baby Revelation

Available now!

HARLEQUIN
Reader Service

Enjoyed your book?

Try the perfect subscription for Romance readers and get more great books like this delivered right to your door.

See why over 10+ million readers have tried Harlequin Reader Service.

Start with a Free Welcome Collection with free books and a gift—valued over $20.

Choose any series in print or ebook.
See website for details and order today:

TryReaderService.com/subscriptions